THE CHINESE
KEYHOLE

THE CHINESE KEYHOLE

RICHARD HIMMEL

CUTTING EDGE

ISBN-13: 978-1-952138-24-9

Published by
Cutting Edge Publishing
PO Box 8212
Calabasas, CA 91372
www.cuttingedgebooks.com

CHAPTER ONE

The thick night hung motionless outside the bedroom window; an unmoving, enveloping curtain of blackness. I was sitting on the edge of the disordered bed, smoking one in a countless chain of cigarettes. There was a mirror across the room. I searched it vacantly, looking past the shadowy darkness of my own nakedness reflected in the foreground of it and seeing the lovely white nakedness of her as she lay behind me.

In the airless warmth of the room there was only one cold, clean object. I held it tightly in my hand, feeling the uncompromising hardness of the small fragment of metal that yesterday had been an instrument of death.

The girl on the bed began to talk again, speaking familiar words punctuated with tears. There was no reason for listening to the words. This that was happening had happened before. I knew the pattern of it, I knew the dialogue of it, and I knew the silences of it. I knew it in a waking state and I knew it in the world of dreams and of half-dreaming. I knew it until I couldn't distinguish the real from the unreal. It was like listening to a record I had heard a thousand times before. It was background music to my own thinking.

It was point and counterpoint in the distance. A picture was in my mind, yesterday's memory. And it was more real than what was happening at that moment.

The smell of the morgue was more vivid than the sweet, pungent perfume of the girl on the bed. The cold, hard light formed an inverted V over the bloodless body on the table. Two doctors

1

worked on the corpse, mechanically and without interest. They had not known the corpse before the blood had been drained out of it, when the corpse had been a man. I had known that man. I was standing back in the shadow of the dark, damp room watching the bullets being extracted one by one from the unsuspecting back. It was hard to watch. I was feeling the pain of each extraction, feeling what the body on the table could not feel. I suppose I looked like a damn fool standing there, alone and untouched, but wincing with pain. I didn't think anyone was watching. If anyone had been, it wouldn't have made any difference. It wasn't the kind of thing I could have disguised.

There were five slugs in his back. After the last one was removed, the young doctor turned toward the darkness where I stood and tossed it to me. I snatched it out of the air and held it in my fist without looking at it.

Later, as he was cleaning up, I walked past the young doctor. My fist had not unclenched; the bullet still lay there, moistened by my sweat and made hot by my blood. "Want it back, Doc?"

He shook his head. "No, I don't think so. They've got enough evidence without it." He began to dry his hands. "I'll tell them it fell to the floor and I couldn't find it. I thought you'd like to keep it."

"Thanks." He lighted a cigarette and offered me one, but I shook my head. "Do me another favor," I said. "Forget I was here, will you?"

"Sure. Are you a relative, a brother or something?"

"He was a guy I knew, that's all. A good guy."

"Any idea how he got it?"

I shrugged my shoulders. "In the back. That's how he got it. That's all I know." I knew more than that. I knew why Tom White had got it, but I couldn't tell. I was going to have to let the police fumble with a crime they would never solve. It was the way it had to be. It was the business I was in. My hands were tied and my lips were sealed.

A tough guy doesn't cry. I wanted to cry because Tom White was dead. But a tough guy doesn't cry. He gets loaded and finds a girl, if he's lucky. Now, twenty-four hours later, my grief had been temporarily expended. In its place there was anger and determination.

The girl had stopped talking.

In the silence that followed there was time to think about the girl. She had been talking about love.

I was thinking I was a dumb, poetic Irish bastard. It would have been so easy to turn to her, take her in my arms, and tell her that I loved her. So easy to kiss her eyes and make the tears stop. To say the words she wanted to hear. So easy.

Except that what I felt for her was not love. It was close to love, as close as a guy can come without loving. I could have said it was love, I could have called it love, I might even have been able to believe it was love if I hadn't known what love really was. But I had known real love once, and I knew that it was something more than a word in a book or a refrain in a song.

Love is when every man part of you is in excitement at once, your brain and your body are one machine functioning simultaneously. It's more than sex. After you've known love, sex without it is flat, not satisfying enough.

I had known that love once, that kind of love. It was different from this. I knew it was right without having to test it and dissect it. It didn't leave me with a hangover of hunger, the unquenchable thirst that I was feeling then. But that girl was gone, that love brief. Ever since she died, the direction of my life was to find that kind of love again. It sent me off on orgiastic tangents, flights of fancy that wound up zero in bed. It had to be sex plus love and love plus sex.

Into the silence of unsaid words came a real sound; the regular, mechanical rhythm of the telephone ringing. I heard it only as a soft noise in the distance, as though it were someone else's phone. I made no move to answer it, nor did she. I only wanted the sound to stop. Finally it did.

"Throw me a cigarette, Johnny."

I looked at her as I threw the pack. I studied her face, seeing the stains that the tears had made. I looked at the firm ripeness of her breasts, the cool perfection of her body. She seemed somehow withdrawn; her body was alone, complete in itself, not needing me.

There was a dryness in my mouth, a parched feeling in my throat, and I too felt alone and empty. But I knew that in time—perhaps a very short time—my wanting for her would return. It would go on and on like this, until I found the other thing, the thing I called love.

There was a gust of smoke from the cigarette and then the sound of her breath emitting it. "What happens now, Johnny?"

I didn't answer. I wanted the silence to continue, I didn't want my own thinking to be distorted. I knew what this thinking, remembering, and indulgent introspection did. It was a device to reinforce passion, to give impetus to the passion. It was a silly substitute for love.

"Nothing happens, does it, Johnny? We go on as we are. I have to stop behaving like a woman in love. Tomorrow you'll walk into my office and I'll be hard as nails again. I'll wisecrack with you and be a real pal. Good old Tina, you'll think. Good old Tina." She laughed a little, and I liked the sound of her laughter, the low, husky sound. It was the sound of the wind whistling low across a deserted city street. "I'll tell you what happens, Johnny. Nothing. Nothing happens until this happens again. I can't stop loving you, Johnny. I can't stop letting you make love to me. That's the way it is."

I wanted to be able to love Tina. As stubbornly as I held onto the memory of every minute I spent with the girl who was dead, I wished just as stubbornly that I had never known her. For if I hadn't known her, I would have thought that this with Tina was what I was looking for, that this was love.

The lust and the will to love were coming back to me. There were the quivering signals of the muscles in my legs; that quick skip-beat of my heart was beginning. If there would have been no tomorrow, I could have said the words "I love you, Tina." But the feel of the discharged bullet in my hand was a reminder that tomorrow would be coming. Tomorrow would begin with harsh sunlight and I would have to be tough again, hard-boiled and hustling. In the daytime I wouldn't remember the hungers that festered inside me that night.

The telephone began to ring again. This time the sound of the ringing was a welcome release.

"Johnny?"

"Who is it?"

"Jacques," the voice said. "What is the matter with you?" I smiled at not recognizing his voice. He had a French accent thick enough to frost pastry with. "Where have you been? I have called before. This is important."

There was the deep sinking feeling in my stomach. "This is important." Maybe, I thought, this is it. Maybe this is what I've been waiting for.

"Just a minute," I said, and turned to Tina. I put my hand over the mouthpiece. "Look, Tina, I'm sorry, but this is ..."

She made it easy for me. "Never mind, Johnny. I'll go powder my nose. Then you can talk sweetly to the lady."

"It's not a lady. This is business. It just happens to be confidential." She walked into the bathroom without saying anything else. I turned back to the phone. "What's up, Jacques?" I lay back on the bed. It was still warm where Tina had been. The fragrance of her was diffused over the pillow.

"It is necessary that I see you at once," Jacques said. "There is a job to be done. It is orders from Biget."

I checked the clock on the dresser. It was almost midnight. The pillow smelled of Tina. Tempting. Maybe it was the chance I was waiting for and maybe it wasn't. "It's awfully late, Jacques." I looked toward the bathroom door. "Can't it wait until tomorrow? I'm kind of—well, tied up."

He laughed. "You should have been a Frenchman, Johnny. Your name should not be Maguire."

"It's a popular pastime among the Irish too, Jacques. Look at all the kids they have."

"You are right," he said. "I am sorry. It is not a French monopoly. But regardless of this, it is most necessary that it be tonight. I have just had word from Biget. I have the instructions for you. I have never before heard you question an order from Biget."

Biget was the code name. It had a variety of meanings. It could mean one man or it could mean headquarters in general. Sometimes it was used as nothing more than a means of identification, a password. Jacques was right, I had never questioned it before. "Where do we meet? Do you want to come here?"

"It is best that I come there. I will knock once, very softly."

"Give me fifteen minutes," I said. "Better make it twenty-five. I've got to have time to get dressed and see the lady home before you get here."

"All right, but make it quick. Very quick."

"Be here at twenty-five past twelve. I'll be ready." Right after I hung up, I wondered if Jacques knew that Tom White was dead. I supposed that he did. Jacques was always in a better position than Tom or me. He always managed to know more.

In a few minutes, Tina came out of the bathroom. I could tell by the way she walked that her passion wasn't expended either, there was still some wanting left in each of us. "I'm sorry, Tina. This is very important. You know that it would have to be for me to leave you now. It's business. Get dressed and I'll run you home."

"Never mind, Johnny. I've got my car. I drove over, remember?" I didn't remember. I was foggy when the evening started. "I suppose," she said, "that I should take a taxi home. It would be more in character. That's the way a call girl operates, isn't it?"

"Stop it, Tina. Don't talk like that. I told you this was important."

"There always seems to be something more important than I." Then a change happened inside her; she eased up and the lines on her face softened. She came over to me, touched my cheek with her fingers quickly, then drew away. "I'm not very understanding, am I, Johnny? I'm sorry, I've been behaving badly. You're upset about something, and I haven't been any help."

"It's okay. I've got shortcomings, too. I know that."

"Most of the time I can look at you and me from your point of view, Johnny; from a man's point of view. Sometimes I forget and carry on like a woman. I have no right to complain about you, really. I'm a big girl and my eyes are wide open. They've been wide open from the beginning. You never tried to fool me about what I meant to you. I like you for that. You're honest. Sometimes you have to put up with my carrying on. It's just that I'm a woman, and women are brought up to believe that when they fall in love, they marry the guy."

I didn't say anything. She was coming out of it. It would be all right by tomorrow. Our relationship would be back to normal.

"It wasn't fair of me," she said, "to make a scene when you're worked up about something else. What is it, Johnny? What's the matter? Do you want to tell me about it?"

The bullet was hot in my hand, as hot as it must have been when it tore the flesh of Tom White's back. Tina was waiting for me to say something. I shook my head. "It's nothing I can talk about, Tina. Forget it. I'll be all right tomorrow."

I watched her as she began to dress. I wished that I could have said to hell with Jacques, to hell with Biget. I wanted to take her now and make love to her as a man in love would do it. But I couldn't say to hell with Biget. That was one job I had to do when they wanted me to do it. My law clients had been different; they could be stalled or ditched and placated later. "If I'm not too late, I'll come up to your place when I'm through."

"Skip it, Johnny. Forget it. I'm tired."

"Come here," I said.

She walked over to the bed and stood in front of me. "What do you want?"

"Closer," I whispered.

I put my arms around her waist and held her close. Her hand ruffed the top of my head, skimmed across the edge of my ear, and made a tingling streak down my spine. The sensation ricocheted through my body. I could feel the hair on my arms stand up. "I don't know why you put up with me." My lips were moving against the softness of her flesh. "I don't know why you go through this all the time. I'm not worth it. Why don't you get a guy who deserves you? Why don't you get a guy with a heart?"

"Because I love you," she said. "Because I love you and someday I'll have you all to myself. You're going to get tired, Johnny. I don't know what you're looking for, I don't know what you're expecting to find. There's something inside you that keeps driving you. You're going to get tired, Johnny. You're going to get tired and give up. All those lovely little hormones of yours are going to sigh and give up. No more chasing after every female in sight. When that happens, you'll come to me and we'll grow old together."

I kissed her. "You're a sap, Tina. You're a hell of a sap."

"Sure, I know that. You're the way you are and I'm a sap. Neither of us can help it. Now, let me go so I can finish dressing." As she wiggled free, my fist unclenched and the bullet dropped to the floor. Tina bent over quickly and picked it up. "What's this, Johnny?"

"What does it look like?"

She studied it for a moment. "It's been shot out of a gun, hasn't it?"

I didn't say anything.

"Is this what you're upset about? Who was it, Johnny?"

"I can't tell you."

She tossed the bullet back to me and turned around. "Was she terribly pretty?"

"It wasn't anything like that. It wasn't a woman. It's just that I can't tell you about it."

"What are you mixed up in, Johnny? You've been so strange lately, so mysterious. Midnight meetings, bullets. Funny things for a lawyer."

"It's not so funny. A lawyer does a lot of things."

"I don't like it, Johnny. I've been worried for a long time. I don't understand it. You're not the type to get mixed up in anything. You've always kept your nose clean before. I can't figure this one out."

"My nose is still clean, Tina. You know I keep on the up-and-up. You know me better than that."

"I guess I know you pretty well. Sometimes I wish you weren't so damned honorable. No one else is when it comes to turning a fast dollar. You have the same opportunities. How many lawyers get rich just sticking to the law?"

"I like it the way it is, Tina. I like being almost poor. There's nothing to love but me this way. Nobody can love me for money or security. It has to be me."

"I don't want you to do anything dishonest, Johnny. This is just business. Listen, you can't be the best damn legal stenographer in town without learning something. I sit in that office of mine all day and listen to lawyers struggle. They don't get rich. If they made big money, they wouldn't use a public stenographic service, and I'd be out of business. But they do take advantage of opportunities. They make more than you and your silly scruples do."

"Look, we've been through this before. I'm happy the way I am. I sleep good at night. I've got enough dough to eat regularly and have fun when I want to. And I'm poor enough so that I can't afford to get married. I think it's a wonderful spot to be in."

She adjusted her hat and peered into the mirror as she smeared on her lipstick. "Johnny?"

"Huh?"

"Whatever it is, this thing you won't tell me about, don't get yourself hurt, will you?"

"I'm pretty good at taking care of myself," I said.

After Tina left, I took a shower and dressed. Then I checked my watch. I had over five minutes until Jacques was due, and Jacques would be on time. Jacques was always on time.

In the six months I had known Jacques Marples, we had become good friends. He was French and what you normally think of as the typical Frenchman. He liked women first, wine second, his work third, and a dog he had owned when he was a kid completed the first division of his interests.

The three of us, Tom White, Jacques, and I, had worked together closely. I got along fine with both Tom and Jacques. They didn't get along too well together, but at least they made a stab at it. Tom and I had been kids together, came out of the same rough neighborhood. Maybe Tom wasn't smart, but he was a sweet guy. He'd give you the shirt off his back.

Tom and I had background in common. Jacques and I, in spite of different nationalities, had interests in common. He talked English very well and my French is okay, so communication between us was easy. He had been a big wheel in the French underground during the war, a really slick espionage man. He was modest about what he had done, but he talked about it a good deal. Our work during the war had been very much alike. As a matter of fact, I spent a stretch working with the underground in southern France.

When I went into the Army, there was a brand-new law degree tacked up on my wall. I figured what the top brass needed more than anything else was a spanking new legal pundit to win the war for them. I used to see the adjutant general's insignia in my sleep. But, as it worked out, that was the only place I saw it, except on other men. I started in the Infantry and after seven months I was transferred to a special assignment.

I had drawn the O.S.S. or the O.S.S. had drawn me. I never figured out which. The boys were going to make a spy out of me, espionage and counterespionage. It happened so fast and I was trained so hard that at first there wasn't much time to figure it out, find out why I happened to get picked.

Very quickly, I learned not to ask questions. In the O.S.S., everything was necessarily secretive. You could learn pieces of things but never an entire story, never what the total picture was all about. The big boys knew, but no one else.

I had a few obvious qualifications for the work. I could speak several languages and speak them without sounding like a touring American. I was particularly good at Italian and a Mexican brand of Spanish. As far back as anyone can remember, there had been nothing in my family but a lot of hard-drinking Irishmen. But I was brought up in a tough neighborhood, a melting pot of Italians, Poles, Mexicans, Puerto Ricans, and what have you. I learned their languages, not the way you learn languages in school, not stilted, archaic, literary construction the way an old-maid schoolteacher speaks it. I learned to speak the way the people around me spoke. I could use the languages and misuse them, cuss in them and make love in them. French was the only language I learned in school, but that came easy. Jacques told me I speak it with a trace of an Italian accent, but anyway it was good enough so that I sounded European, not American.

My appearance must have been part of it, too. I'm not the picturesque kind of Irishman, not red-haired and green-eyed. My hair is dark and my eyes are dark, and when I worked up a good sweat I could pass as a southern European. That meant a lot in the behind-the-lines work I did.

The amateur boxing I had done was on my record, too; they knew about that. My talent with a well sharpened pocket knife was something they found out later. It was by far the most useful weapon I ever carried.

I had a hell of a time in the war. Both good and bad. It was exciting and dull. Some of it was dangerous, very dangerous. But the experiences I had could never be shared with anyone, they could never be told. Even after the war, what I had done was still not to be talked about. No one ever knew what I was doing. No one who addressed a letter to me c/o Postmaster could have guessed that I was standing, maybe, in a line of Italian peasants, trying to learn something or trying to pick off a key collaborator. Or I would be in India, maybe. Or France. I was in many places during the war, doing many things, being many different people.

After it was over and there was no excitement any more, I remembered the shiny new law degree. I remembered the dreams I had had when I was a kid, dreams of being a lawyer and being the man a kid thinks a lawyer is. I didn't have any problems readjusting. I had something to do. I was going to be the hottest lawyer in town; clean and tough, honest and fearless. Mr. District Attorney was going to look like small-time stuff compared to me.

Things didn't work out the way I planned. It isn't easy to set a town on its ear, particularly a big city. Young lawyers returning from service were as thick as bedbugs crawling out of woodwork. I had a couple of strikes against me. I wasn't one of the fancy-school boys. I came up the hard way. I came from a background where the rule was to break the law, not to defend it and interpret it. I had to grab my schooling when I could, mostly at night. It was sporadic schooling when I had the dough. I made money by working with my hands, construction crews, subway digging, all kinds of backbreaking work.

But I found out that an old school tie goes a lot farther in the legal world than calloused hands. I started by looking for a job with a big, well-established firm. No dice. I may have been bright and I may have been determined, but I was a foul ball. I was wrong side of the tracks and wrong school. I'm not blaming anyone; there were thousands looking for jobs. The big outfits took the men from the big schools. It was a policy, and that was that.

So I said nuts to the fancy boys, I was going to do it on my own. I opened my own office and hustled for clients. It was rough. It wasn't the law. It didn't have a thing to do with the kind of law I had dreamed about when I was a kid.

There were chances to crack big-time operations, shady deals for shady people. But I said nuts to those things, too. I was going to be the kind of lawyer I wanted to be or no lawyer at all.

One day an average-looking guy came into my office and offered me a job doing espionage work again. He was with the State Department. It wasn't too much money for the risks, but when he said the word "espionage" that feeling shot down the center of my back and I could taste some of the old excitement. I looked at the four office walls that I had been knocking my head against, at the file cabinet I had so carefully selected and used so little.

I gave myself some hogwash about being a patriot, but that was only part of it. The money would come in regularly, I wouldn't have to sweat out the rent every month. That had a lot to do with it. Most of all, I felt the restlessness beginning inside me. My hands clenched into fists and I remembered how good it felt to slug someone. The muscles in my legs got hard and I remembered running for my life down a narrow Egyptian street.

The deal with the State Department was fairly clean-cut. I was to keep my law office and use it as a front. I could take cases now and then, as part of the camouflage. Outside of that, I didn't know anything. The man said that I would be contacted. I sat for three weeks before somebody showed up.

That man was Jacques Marples. He was my contact man. It was through him that I received my instructions.

We hit it off right away. "How come," I asked him that first day, "you came to this country to do this work?"

He smiled and shrugged his shoulders. "In France it is very dull. Everybody is a spy. One day everybody is against something and the next day everybody is on the side of the same thing. It is very dull. There is no excitement."

"How did you land over here?"

"I have friends," he told me. "I have friends whom I have known in France. They know the work that Jacques Marples has done for his country in the underground. They know that he is very fast and very quick." He blushed a little and lowered his head. "I say this only because it is true. I am born for this work. It is in the blood. You too, no?"

"I'm not sure," I said. "I like to eat regularly. That has something to do with it."

"It is very useful for your country to have me. I have many friends in France. They tell me many things when it is necessary to know them. I know also many things in this country. Women," he said, "already I know many. More than I have need for. If, at any time, you wish to trade information, we can arrange it discreetly, is it not?"

Boy, he knew some lulus, too. I thought my supply line was good. Where he found all those janes, I don't know. He had them every which way, any way you wanted them.

Unfortunately, it was impossible for Jacques and me to be seen together anywhere. Our meetings were always behind closed doors. It was too bad. I always figured he'd be good company on a bender. But being seen with him was definitely against regulations and dangerous.

Tom White was struggling around, working in an office. When it came time to get additional help, I got Tom White. It was routine work but he liked it and I could trust him.

For six months we had been working hard to crack an organization that was smuggling atomic information out of the country. We were small parts of the big counterespionage machine. We were never told the whole picture or even given a whole job to do. It was always pieces of things, parts of the big job. But I had been on enough assignments to know pretty much what was going on.

The big leak was coming from two universities in our area and from one atomic plant. The information was coded through the city and passed into Red China, and from there God knows where. We had our suspicions. I had been able to smoke out an agent here and there, but the big brains of the organization were untouched. The small fry that we had been able to put the finger on were left alone most of the time. They weren't important. If we eliminated them, they would only be replaced. The instructions were to leave them where we found them, the strategy being that sooner or later there would be a slip-up and one of them would lead us to the chief of the spy ring. Once the key man was eliminated, the entire structure beneath him would collapse.

I was tired of doing pieces of the job. I wanted the assignment to do the big job. Get the brains. That's what I wanted my superiors to tell me to do. I wanted it maybe for the promotion it would have meant if I was successful. Promotion and more dough. But I wanted it, too, because that's the way I'm built. I have to follow through

Now I was more anxious than ever to get the assignment. I had a score to settle for Tom White. I knew that I would never rest until I found the guy who gave it to him. And when I found that person, he was going to get five slugs. But not in the back, not the way he did it to Tom. He was going to see what was coming. He was going to feel them go into his belly. One by one.

They had got Tom that night instead of me. That was part of the reason for feeling the way I did. That and because I liked Tom. He was a good guy. He got it in the back. That's no way to get it. In any business. For any reason.

Last night a message had come through to do a job. It seemed a routine assignment, nothing big or out of the ordinary. I had a date and Tom didn't. He said that since he didn't have any plans he might as well do it. So Tom got it instead of me.

My hands were tied by regulations. To go off on my own and track down Tom's killer was strictly forbidden. I was to do only what I was instructed to do. But if I were given the big job, that would mean that I would give the orders, I would make my own plans and decisions. Then I could find the killer. Then I could even it up for Tom. It's the thing he would have done for me.

Promptly at twelve-twenty-five there was a soft knock on the door.

I had that feeling in my stomach. Maybe this was it. Maybe this was the big job to do. "Come in."

Jacques poked his head in the door. "The lady," he said, "she is gone?"

"Yeah, she's gone. Come on in, Jacques."

"I was thinking after I talked to you on the telephone that it is too bad to make the lady leave. I should have offered to keep her company while you were gone. It would have been most polite, no?"

"It would have been most polite, definitely no."

"It is very bad that I must break up the affair, Johnny. I am sorry."

"Forget it. What's up? What's the job? The big one, maybe?"

Jacques looked down and shook his head. He knew how much I wanted it. He knew how much I had wanted it before this thing happened to Tom. "The message said that it is important, but it is not what you want."

"You know about Tom, don't you?"

"*Oui.* I was not certain that you did."

"I saw him, Frenchie. Dead. Dead as anything you've ever seen. In the back. I'll square things off for Tom if it's the last thing I do. I swear it. If they don't give me the big job, I'll quit the department and do it on my own, no matter what happens to me."

"You were good friends, you and Tom. What happened is—how can I say it?—it is part of this business, our business. Tomorrow, maybe, you will feel a little better. You will see that it is not wise to sacrifice everything for a man you can no longer help. In the heart it makes sense, yes. But up here," he tapped his head, "it is not smart."

"I don't live from up there, Jacques. I live from here, from the heart. Maybe I'm a sucker, but that's the way I am."

"I hope for the sake of your heart that you get the big job, Johnny."

"Thanks, Jacques. I know you do."

"Now, you must go quickly. It is a small thing but you must go at once."

"What am I supposed to do?"

"First, I have brought for you the present." He handed me a box wrapped as a gift. You could tell that it was a necktie two blocks away.

"Thanks very much. What's the occasion?"

"Open it."

I opened it, and sure enough, it was a tie, and not a very pretty one. It was hand-painted on silk, a very modern design with all sorts of gimmicky lines and free forms. On the back there was a label that said it was pure silk and made in France. "It looks swell, Jacques. Thanks a lot." I started to put it back in the box.

"You do not like it and it is not a present. Put it on. You must wear it."

I looked at the tie again. The gimmicky lines and forms were code. I don't know why I hadn't figured that out right away. I was going to carry a message that definitely did not match my socks. As I was putting it on I said, "Where do I go and what do I do?"

"From Biget I have received the instructions," he began. I never asked Jacques who his contact was, who the man was who issued my instructions. It was against regulations to tell any names or to give any information to another agent except that which was specified. "You are to wear the tie and you are to go to the Chinese Keyhole." He spoke slowly as he pronounced the name. "You know what that is, Johnny, this Chinese Keyhole? I do not."

"Sure. It's a strip-tease joint in Chinatown. It caters to the visiting firemen. You know, the tourist crowd, conventioneers. They take you for everything you've got. It's one of the most famous clip joints in this part of the country. What am I supposed to do there?"

"You are to go there and to sit at a table and it will happen to you."

"What will happen to me?"

Jacques smiled and his shoulders made their characteristic shrug. "*Qui sait,* Johnny? Who knows?"

On the surface it looked like a snap job. I could get back to Tina in no time at all. All it looked like was a straight job of delivering a message coded on a tie. Only a few things puzzled me. It was imperative that it be done that night, so it must have been important. And they were sending me on a job that looked like a breeze. That wasn't like Biget. I usually drew the bloody, dirty jobs. It appeared easy, but I was suspicious.

"Is that all there is to it?"

"That is all I know."

"What do you think, Jacques? You think it's part of the same deal?"

"Who knows, Johnny? Maybe it is yes and maybe it is no. You know how this business is. It is the Chinese Keyhole, but it may mean nothing. And then it may mean something. You know how it is."

"You're pretty good at smelling this stuff out. Do you think it's going to be simple tonight, the way it looks?"

"With us it is never easy. It looks simple, as you say. It is maybe yes. Then, on the other hand ..."

I took off my coat, slipped on my shoulder holster, took my knife, and put it in my pocket. "I guess you can't ever tell," I said. "Somehow it always gets rough before it's over."

"It is most likely just the routine, Johnny."

"Most likely." I patted my gun and adjusted the tie. "Okay, I guess this is it."

"You go ahead, Johnny. I will wait for a while to leave."

"If there isn't any brandy left in the bottle, I've got a new one in the cabinet under the sink."

"Johnny?"

"Yes?"

"You will tell me if it is good, this Chinese Keyhole? Maybe I go there some night. You tell me."

"I'll scout for you. If there's anything that looks like your type. I'll let you know. Good night, Jacques."

"Good luck, Johnny."

"Thanks."

It was a good night, the way nights are at the end of summer. There was a cool undercurrent in the wind, foreshadowing the autumn that was coming. I got into my car, started the engine, and then looked up at the windows, of my apartment. All the lights were out. Jacques, I knew, was still there, watching me from the window, drinking my brandy in the darkness.

I thought a little about the Chinese Keyhole as I began driving away. Their shows had a hell of a reputation. Pretty raw, very naked. It was a lousy spot to be sending a guy who was still feeling as horny as I was.

CHAPTER TWO

It had been a long time since I had been to Chinatown. The color and Oriental-squalor kind of charm was gone. The main street was edged on both sides with dirty, decaying buildings; symbols everywhere of the filth, neglect, and poverty of the city. And looming up at the far end of the street was the giant electric sign spelling out Chinese Keyhole, first in red and then in yellow lights. A red and gold glass pagoda facade had been superimposed on an old brownstone building. There was a red canopy extending from the entrance to the street.

A big man with Mongoloid features opened the door for me. He was done up in a mandarin costume, also red with many gold embellishments. As soon as the door opened, I caught the heavy smell of incense. The odor was not heavy enough to outweigh the smell of stale, unwashed air.

A cute little Chinese girl with a flower in her hair was at the check room. But the man who showed me to a table was not Chinese. His nationality was bouncer. All over the world these men looked alike to me; nationality, bouncer.

The main room was long and narrow, the walls on each side draped in heavy, cheap yellow satin. At the far end there was a stage with a pagoda-shaped proscenium arch and a long runway coming from the center of the stage almost as far back as the entrance. Circular tables were huddled close together on either side of the runway. It was dark and smoky. An off-stage orchestra was playing typical burlesque music, tinny-sounding except for the occasional breaking through of the clarinetist, who knew his music and deserved to be blowing in better company.

On the stage, a redheaded tomato was going through the last motions of her strip act. I looked at the dimly illuminated placard next to the stage. It said, "Violet, Danseuse Parisienne." As I sat down at one of the tables, Violet pulled the last rip cord and the remaining fragment of flimsy chiffon floated away. Violet was as God had made her. With one exception. A bunch of artificial violets hung at the meeting of her legs. The act was lousy and I had seen better than Violet without paying good money for it. Even in the condition I was in, she left me cold.

The waitress who came over to the table was dressed in an abbreviated kimono job that exposed a lot of legwork. There was a sequin-trimmed coolie hat plunked on top of her head. But between the coolie hat and the top of the kimono was strictly the map of Ireland. She looked a little bit like my cousin in Pittsburgh.

"What'll it be, mister?"

"A bottle of Tavern Pale."

"You look like you can handle something stronger than beer."

I looked up to see if she were looking at my tie. I couldn't be sure. She was writing something on her order pad. "Beer will be fine," I said. "The only thing stronger I want to handle is something like you."

Her expression didn't change. These girls got plenty of lip from plenty of guys. I managed to get a squint at the pad she had been writing on. All it said was "Tavern Pale." She muttered something and walked away. I turned back to watch the redhead grind out her curtain call.

After some scattered applause, a voice came through the microphone announcing the next act. "And now, the most sensational act in the history of the theatre. Presenting Gail Nevaire in the Dance of the White Goddess and the Slave Girls."

The lights blacked out completely and the off-stage music began again. It was scarcely audible at first, but it built in intensity and volume. There was the clean, wonderful sound of the clarinet coming through the Oriental honky-tonk music. The curtains opened slowly and an overhead spot came up gradually, timed to grow brighter with the increasing volume of the music. When it was in full brightness, it was shining on the biggest blonde I ever saw.

Standing motionless in the center of the stage, she was stark naked, dazzling white. She was six feet tall, easy. Around her waist there was a thick iron belt, and from the belt ran six heavy chains. Then, slowly, a lute-sounding instrument plucked out a counterpoint theme with the band and purple sidelights came up around the stage.

At the end of each iron chain there was a naked girl, bound to the chain by an iron belt like that worn by the big blonde. These girls were Orientals, small with wonderful tawny-colored skin, tight bodies seeming even smaller in contrast to the Statue of Liberty proportions of the big blonde. They were doing all the dancing, if you could call it dancing. Their bodies moved in syrupy undulations. The big blonde didn't do a thing but pivot around in the center of the stage and crack a long whip into the air.

It was a hell of an act. It reached out and caught me and held me hard. My eyes couldn't waver and my thoughts couldn't stray. Everyone in the place must have felt the same way. It was as though a secret, perverted part of you had come to the surface to tantalize and excite you, to hold you spellbound. I had forgotten what I was supposed to be doing there.

How long it went on, I'm not sure. I lost track of time. The effect was druglike. I was drugged until a flash of lightning bolted on the stage. It came suddenly and with a whipping sound. In the center of it there was a figure leaping through the air, a long, muscular body covered with bronze paint.

He was big, bigger than the blonde, and he was one hell of a good dancer. He danced around the slave girls, holding a large key, freeing them from their shackles one by one. When they were all unlocked, he went to work on the big blonde, grasping the whip from her hand and letting it lash with a fury. His body was coordinated with the snaky movements of the whip. He was dancing but it was more than dancing; some of the lashes were hitting the blonde. I could see red marks beginning to appear on her body. She just stood there, stone like and impassive, taking the beatings of the whip. Then the music became faster, and when everything seemed to be climaxing, it stopped abruptly. The male dancer fell to the floor, breathing heavily, breathing quickly, breathing to the rhythm of sexual exhaustion. And each breath was punctuated with the plucking sound of the lute, slower and softer until his breathing was not apparent and there was no sound and then there was the darkness again.

No one applauded. It wasn't the kind of thing to applaud. I saw a couple of guys mop their foreheads and reach for a drink. It made you want a drink the worst way. I ordered another bottle of beer. It took that and about fifteen minutes before I was back to normal and remembered that I had a job to do, I had a message to deliver. I still didn't know to whom.

About that time, the performers came from backstage to mingle with the customers and get drinks bought for them. The six Chinese slave girls came out with the rest. They wore short kimonos and had nothing on underneath. They made no effort to keep the things closed. I was alone, obviously on the prowl. I was ready bait. A little Chinese girl came over and looked me up and down. "Lonesome?" she asked. I made a quick survey of what she had to offer. I was thinking, Honey, the way I feel now, it's me for you and you for me.

"Keep moving," I muttered. "Get going." She shrugged her shoulders and the kimono opened wider. Man! But I was on a job. It was hard to keep my mind on my work, but I had to. In a couple of minutes another one came over. She was just as good-looking as the first. I don't know, maybe anything would have looked good to me at that point.

"Want company, mister?"

"Scram, baby. Keep moving."

"We could have fun," she said. "I like you. I like the way you look. I like your tie. It's very pretty."

"Sit down."

This time she whispered. "She's watching. Say no again, very loud."

"No!"

"Something is wrong. I can't stay here. Everything is about to break. The blonde knows. We must save it. Two-six-two-five Mason Street. Meet me there later. Make sure that you are not followed. They know about me. Two-six-two-five Mason Street. C. Wong."

Then her voice picked up. "You don't know how much fun a Chinese girl can be, mister."

"You heard me. I said to keep moving." She walked away. I tried to follow her out of the corner of my eye, but I lost her in the half darkness of the room. I made sure that the address was well planted in my mind. I ordered another drink and sat back to relax and wait.

Things were getting interesting. I was thinking that maybe my feeling for this business was getting away from me. Last night it had looked like a routine assignment and now Tom dead from it. The little Chinese girl had said, "Everything is about to break." There was more here than I bargained for. I was telling myself that maybe this was it, maybe this was the big job. From where I was sitting I couldn't be sure. I had to bide my time, watch every movement around me. That included the big blonde. I heard her voice before I looked up to see her.

"What's the matter, mister, no likee the Chinese stuff?"

"Sit down," I said. "I'll buy you a drink."

She was good-looking, if you go for that supersized stuff. She was dressed in a white sparkling formal that was cut down in front to her hips. There was a black pearl set into her navel. The waitress came over and we ordered drinks.

"You didn't answer my question," she said. "Why don't you like Chinese girls?"

"I'm a straightforward guy. I just don't like 'em. How did you guess?"

She smiled. "I've been watching you. You turned two of them away."

"How come you've been watching me? Is there anything special about me?"

She looked me up and down. She was a girl who knew what she wanted. "You're my size," she said.

"How can you tell?"

"You're cute." She laughed a little. "You're real cute."

The drinks came and she had swallowed hers before the waitress left the table. "Bring me another." The waitress looked at me. I shook my head. "Just make it one for the lady."

"That last Chink was giving you a rough time, wasn't she? She was very persistent. What kind of a line was she feeding you?"

"Same old routine," I said. "She said that she was tired of sitting with old, worn-out hardware salesmen. She said that I looked intelligent, like a man she could talk to." I shrugged my shoulders. "Who wants to talk?"

The blonde seemed relieved and satisfied with my explanation. "She's right about you. You're slumming. You're not like the other guys here. You're out seeing how the other half lives."

"How do they live?"

"Upstairs," she said. "I have an apartment upstairs."

"I said *how* do they live, not where."

"Not interested?"

"I didn't say that. Maybe. It depends. How come you live upstairs?"

"Why not?"

"I don't know. You seem like the fancy kind, swell hotel, French maid."

"It's more convenient upstairs. You see, I own the biggest piece of this joint."

I was tempted to make a wisecrack, but I let it pass.

"Well, what do you say?"

"I said it depends."

"On what?"

"How come you want me? Do I look like I've got dough? I haven't. Not the kind of dough that would make any sense to you."

"I didn't say anything about money, did I?"

"Love? Is this going to be for love?"

"Why not?" She lit a cigarette.

"I'm always a man ready to take advantage of any opportunity, but this one overwhelms me. I don't know why you picked me out."

"How tall are you?"

"Six three and a half."

"I get tired of looking around for what's in bed with me. You won't get lost so easy."

I laughed and she laughed too. "We'll see," I said.

"The last show is over in an hour. Ask the doorman. He'll show you the way up."

The man she had danced with came over to the table and sat down. The bronze paint was off except for flecks of it at his hairline and around his mouth. I was thinking that if she wanted to go to bed with something big, this guy looked like her meat. He was plenty big and had a good build, but his face was weak, too damn pretty. Ten to one he was as queer as a three-dollar bill.

She turned to him. "What do you want?"

"Charlie wants to see you." His voice was soft and very definitely swish.

"You go tell Charlie to wait. I'll talk to him when I get good and ready." She was mad. The ballet dancer was giving me the eye. I didn't like the looks of that one. Okay, so he was queer, but he still had the size and muscles to knock the hell out of a guy. And, I figured, the disposition for it. "Go on, Pete, get away from here," she said.

"Tell your friend that maybe he ought to leave," the ballet boy said. "You know how mad Charlie gets when you play up to another guy."

"To hell with Charlie," the blonde said. "I want another drink." Then she turned to me. "You've got it clear about later, haven't you?"

I nodded. None of us said anything for a few minutes after the drinks came. Pete got his down in one dainty gulp. "Okay, Pete, you've had your drink, now go tell Charlie to keep his shirt on until I get there."

He stood up and held out his hand. I shook it. He was powerful, all right. "If you know what's good for you, fellow, you'll stay away from her. Charlie gets so mad. She's always on the make but Charlie won't let her. Remember that. Or we'll meet again and it won't be so pleasant. Not the way I'd like it to be." He winked.

I sat down without saying anything. He stood behind the blonde and leaned down, whispering something in her ear.

"What's the difference?" she said. "It's got to be done, and it's got to be done before it's too late. Charlie knows that. You handle it your way. You've got to be good for something."

"Don't forget, dear," he said to her, "there's a business meeting later. You-know-who is coming and it's important. Don't get carried away by your friend." He looked over at me again. " 'By."

"Nice kid," I said. "A very pleasant type."

"He makes me sick. I need another drink." I signaled to the waitress. "He's the only one Charlie will trust me with. He stays as close to me as a girdle. I can't have any fun. What's the use of having dough if you can't have fun? Three shows a night I do. I knock myself out. For what? Sure, I can buy things, but Charlie won't let me go nowhere, he won't let me see nobody. Only him and that fruit." The drink came and she took it quickly. Her tongue was loose and fast. "If I wasn't in so deep I'd throw it all over." She snapped her fingers. "Just like that. That's how much I think of all this. You can have the dough. It's no good if you can't have any fun. I never have any fun."

"It seems to me that if I tried to get up to see you after the show, I'd have trouble."

"You scared?"

"Not scared. Cautious, maybe. I'm used to my face the way it is. I don't want it pushed in."

"You see what I mean? It's always like this. I never can do anything I want to do. You see the doorman when you leave. He's my friend. He'll get you upstairs without anybody seeing you. There won't be any trouble."

"I don't know." I said. "I'll see."

She leaned over and whispered something in my ear.

There was some noise behind me and a lot of Chinese jabber. I looked up and there was a man about five-two standing at the table, running off his mouth and waving his arms at the blonde. It was hard to tell how old he was; Chinese people look young for a long time. It gave me a charge to think about the blonde and this guy in bed together. He was throwing Chinese at her a mile a minute. Finally she stood up and walked past him. "Aw, shut up," she said.

"You like the show, mister?"

"It's good. Good show."

"Better to watch from where you are sitting. Much safer there." He looked like a character in the last reel of a Charlie Chan movie. He waddled as he walked away.

The blonde was standing at the door leading backstage. She was trying to tell me something. All I caught was "I'll see you later." Not if I see you first, baby, I thought. She didn't do a thing to me. Too big, maybe. Too much of everything.

Besides, there wasn't time. I had to finish my job. I had to find out about the little Chinese girl. I wanted to get my message delivered and get going.

After two more drinks the show started and I signaled the waitress to bring my check. My bill was over twenty dollars for a few lousy drinks. It would be charged on my expense account so I didn't put up a stink; besides, I wanted to get out as quietly as possible. I got past the check-room girl without any trouble. But outside the doorman stopped me. "Miss Nevaire's apartment is right at this next entrance. I'll show you the way. It's clear now. Nobody will know."

"Never mind. Tell Miss Nevaire I'm not in the mood. Tell her maybe some other time. Maybe later."

"I got orders," he said. "When the boss gives orders, I follow them."

There was time to size up the situation and time to size up him. I wasn't worried about holding my own with him. I figured I could handle him all right. But if he got tough, there was going to be a fight, and a fight meant noise and a crowd. I wanted to exit unnoticed. I wanted to get to the address on Mason Street without being followed. I took out my wallet, pulled out a five spot, and gave it to him. "Look, General, I don't feel like it now. Did you ever just not feel like it? You go up there and tell her I'll be back later."

With his left hand he pocketed the bill and with his right hand he telegraphed what was coming. Luckily, the drinks hadn't been too strong; my sense of timing was still intact. I ducked and caught him just right, throwing him over my shoulder and onto the sidewalk. With the butt of my gun I clonked him over the head, rolled him over to take the five bucks out of his pocket, made a beeline for my car, and got out of there as fast as I could.

I kept watching through the rear-view mirror to see if any-one were following. Maybe I was being too careful. In my busi-ness, you can't be too careful. As far as I knew, the blonde had no suspicions. It was a pure case of body versus body. But I couldn't take chances. I went back to the apartment, parked the car, went upstairs, lighted the lamp in the bedroom, and stood in the dark-ened living room watching the street below.

For five minutes there was no sign of anyone. Then from across the street a small figure appeared in the shadows. When the figure stopped at the curb and was in the light of the lamp-post, I saw it was a woman, huddled in a big coat. She was hatless and unsteady. She seemed to be looking directly at my window. She walked across the street straight to the entrance of the build-ing. There was something familiar about her, but the light was too dim for me to identify her.

There are eighty apartments in the building. She could have been going into any one of them, but then the buzzer sounded from downstairs. I pressed the button, drew my gun, and waited.

The knock came weakly on the door.

"Who is it?"

"Johnny. Johnny, let me in." The voice was a tired, frantic whisper.

"Who is it?"

"Leona. It's Leona, Johnny. Let me in, let me in." She was pounding on the door, but the sound was strengthless, gloved and weary.

I knew then who it was. The brief glimpse of her under the light and the speaking of her name went together. But I didn't know why she was outside my door. Why now, after all this time? I opened the door cautiously, not putting away my gun. She fell, more than came, into the room.

"Where is he, Johnny? What's happened to him?" She sat on the couch. The only light in the room was coming from the bed-room. She was thinner. Her hair had grown back to its natural mousy color. It hung in thick strings from her head, uncombed. Her head was down in her hands and through the thickness of the coat I could see that she was shivering. I poured a drink and handed it to her. She shook her head.

"Go on," I said. "It'll do you good."

"No, don't make me. Please don't make me. Please, Johnny. Please."

The girl was near hysteria. I held her head back and poured the drink down her mouth. She resisted at first, but when enough of it got in to warm her, she swallowed the remainder hungrily. "Give me another, Johnny."

I poured another drink. This time she took it herself and drank it in one gulp. It steadied her.

"Something has happened to him, hasn't it?"

"What are you talking about? Who?"

"Tom. Where is he? What's happened to him?"

This was something new, Leona and Tom. I hadn't known about it. She had been my girl for a while, a few years back. She was a lively bleached blonde then. Full of fun, a hell of a drinker.

"What has Tom got to do with you?"

She stood up and poured another drink for herself. "It's all right, Johnny. I'm—I'm fine now. Just fine. You can tell me. It's all right. Really. Go ahead. Tell me what's happened to him."

It wasn't all right, I knew that. But it was no secret that Tom was dead. She would have to know. I told her straight out. She flinched. Once. She grabbed the bottle. Just holding it seemed to be giving her strength and warmth.

"I knew it," she said. "I knew it was going to happen."

"How did you know?"

She was looking at the bottle. I nodded to her to go ahead and drink. "It was too good to last, Tom and me. It was too good, he was too good a guy to live. They don't let good guys live in this world, Johnny. They're not tough enough. They're too sweet. They're too wonderful."

"It must have been more than that. You must have known something definite to believe that he was dead."

She shook her head. "No, Johnny. I don't know what Tom did. He never told me. But I knew there was danger. You can tell in a guy's eyes. Did you ever study people's eyes? You can tell so much by looking into eyes. Tom's eyes were blue. Clear blue. Like Technicolor pictures of lakes you see in travelogues in the movies." She drank again. When she spoke her voice was lower. "He didn't come to me last night. He was supposed to. He didn't show up all day and again tonight. There had to be something wrong. He wouldn't run out on me, not now."

"I didn't know," I said. "I didn't even know that you two knew each other."

"Funny how we met, Johnny. It was because of you. Isn't that funny? It was because of you. I was broke and I was beaten. I was a lush." She looked at the glass and laughed. "A real, honest-to-goodness lush. I was no good for anything. Nobody wanted me around. I used to be fun on a party. Do you remember, Johnny? Remember all the good times we used to have? I wasn't like that after a while. I drank too much, got drunk too quick. I slobbered and passed out. No one wanted me. I wasn't any fun. So I came to you, Johnny, to your office, because I needed help. Maybe all I wanted to do was bum enough dough to buy a bottle, I don't know. I came to you because as tough as you talk, you're a guy with a heart. But you weren't there. Tom was."

She stopped talking, looked at the bottle, and then back at me. "You know something? This is the first time I've had anything to drink in four months. Tom felt sorry for me that day. He took me out and bought me a meal. He wouldn't buy me a drink. After the meal he took me up to his apartment. I didn't care. I wanted money to buy booze. But nothing happened. He talked to me. Can you imagine that? Going up to a guy's room and listen to him talk all night." She smiled. "I was awful. I screamed and carried on something awful. Just for a drink. I couldn't believe what I was listening to. Tom was saying things about a woman's self-respect. About living a good life. About how there was a chance for me. At first I thought maybe he was some crackpot reformer; a nut, a screwball. But he was too much of a man for that, I could tell. You know what he did the next morning?"

She waited for me to say something, but I didn't.

"The next morning he took me in for the cure. Not that dump the city runs. This place was clean and they were nice to you and they treated you like a lady, not a broken-down drunk. The sun came in my window every morning. Like it did in my room when I was a kid. Tom came too. Just as regular as the sun. He brought me things to eat and things to read. He paid for the whole works. I never could figure out how much it cost him. Plenty, I think.

"When I got well enough, he took me out of there and got a little apartment for me. I was doing fine. I was going to get a job. I fell in love with him, Johnny. Can you imagine that, me in love? Like a kid falls in love. Like I was sixteen years old. And you want to know something else, Johnny? Tom didn't love me. He didn't want nothing from me. He only wanted to give. He only wanted to help. He didn't want nothing for himself. He was that kind of guy."

I walked back to the window. "Yes," I said, "he was that kind of guy."

"I loved him, Johnny," she whispered. "There will never be anyone like him again. He was too good to be true. Too good to be alive, I guess."

"What are you going to do, Leona?"

"Remember him," she said. "As long as I live, I'll remember him."

"I'm sorry about making you take the drink. I didn't know."

"It's all right, Johnny. It doesn't make any difference. I don't think I want any more now. Maybe it's a good thing I drank what I did. Before—before I took the cure, I could never stop. I'd have had the whole bottle down me by now. But I'm not going to drink any more now. I don't have to be afraid."

"What about dough? I don't think Tom had much. He was supporting his old lady. She'll get the insurance money."

"I'll get along all right, Johnny. My rent's paid up and he socked a little in a bank account for me. What about you?"

"What do you mean, what about me?"

"What are you going to do?"

"I don't know what you're getting at."

"You were kids together, weren't you? Been pals a long time. You were a big brother to him. You're going to miss that, Johnny. You're going to miss him."

"Maybe."

"You know who did it?"

I shook my head.

"I knew you pretty well, Johnny. We had some good times together." I heard her turn the doorknob. I kept looking out the window. Maybe I didn't want her to see my face. Maybe there were some tears there. "Johnny," she said, "when you square it up for Tom, when you get even for him, give the guy that did it something extra, will you? Make it something extra for me."

There was the sound of the door opening and the sound of the door closing. I was alone. I rubbed my hand across my eyes. Tears became mingled with the sweat.

CHAPTER THREE

A cold spot of fear burned the pit of my stomach. I don't care how many times a guy goes through danger, he never gets used to it. Sometimes you can control yourself so that your hand doesn't shake, so that your shoulders are broad and your jaw is square. But you can't do anything about that other feeling, the cold spot.

It was there, ringing danger alarms throughout my nervous system, as I rode in a cab toward the address the little Chinese girl had given me. I got out two blocks away and walked the rest of the distance through the dark, vacant streets.

A dim light burned in the entryway of the building on Mason Street; except for that, there was no light anywhere. I checked my watch; there had been plenty of time for the Chinese girl to finish the last show and get back to the apartment. In the vestibule there was a faint smell of spoiled garbage. I looked at the names on the mailboxes. A couple were Chinese and a few were Mexican. I pressed the buzzer next to "C. Wong" and waited.

Nothing happened.

I pressed it again, a long hard ring this time, but still nothing happened. There was a good chance that the bell wasn't working. There was just as good a chance that something had happened to her. I was on my guard. This was no kid's game; these boys played rough.

There were no apartment numbers next to the names, so I tried to figure out the location of C. Wong's apartment from the position of the mailboxes. I was sure it was on the second floor. I walked through the dirty hall and up the squeaking staircase.

The building originally had been three large flats, one on each floor, but it had been cheaply remodeled so now there were three apartments on each floor. I had my choice of three doors. None of them had a name. While I was in the middle of the hall scratching my head, I hoard the slight squeaking sound of a door. Quickly I backed up into the shadows. One of the doors had opened a crack. I was being watched. My hand was on my gun, ready. Then, from the bottom of the door, a hand strained forward, trying to pull the door open. There was a moaning sound coming from the apartment. It was a woman's hand, small and with long painted fingernails.

I whispered the word "Biget."

One finger made a forced sign, beckoning me. I drew the gun and walked to the door. I tried to push it open but it was blocked; there was something in the way. Now I moved fast, forcing the door open, and in doing so I heard a girl cry out in pain. I flicked on the light switch. The Chinese girl lay on the floor. Half of her clothes were torn off, and there were great, bleeding gashes all over her body. Her tiny face was twisted and distorted with pain. Her eyes were open and pleading.

I looked around the room and there were signs of a terrific struggle. One window was open and the night air blew in, billowing the threadbare lace curtains. I went to the window and looked out. It was a good jump to the fire escape. I turned back to the tortured body. "Through here?"

She tried to say something but only pained sounds came from her throat. She nodded to indicate that whoever had been there had left through the window. Below me, the alley was desolate, no sign of life. The ringing of the bell had scared off the intruder. It had to be the ballet dancer. The marks of the whip were symbols of his handicraft. The jump from the window to the fire escape was a broad one, but he could have made it in a quick leap. My hands ached to push that classical face of his in. I had reason now, a hell of a good motive for mayhem. When the time came, and I knew that the time would be coming, it would give me great pleasure to belt his muscled belly and kick his poetic ass. One thing I knew, that was not the killer who had knocked off Tom. The handiwork was different, the technique of the amateur. The man or woman who killed Tom had acted quickly to get results. This was the work of someone who got a charge out of killing. My inning with him would come. The poor beat-up girl came first.

I picked her up as carefully as I could and carried her to the couch. I've seen a lot of suffering. I've seen guys with a belly full of bullets, with pieces of their bodies torn off. But they didn't have anything on her. She was a goner, I knew that. She had been beaten until parts of her body looked like something in a butcher shop. She would have to be like this, suffering like this, until God was merciful enough to blank her out, to let her die.

There was nothing I could do for her. I had to remind myself that the important thing was to find out where to go next, who was the next person in the chain. My job was to deliver a message; I couldn't forget that. There wasn't time to behave like a human being.

She had hold of my arm and her nails dug deep into me with every wave of pain. She was forcing herself to hold consciousness. She had her job to do, too.

"Take it easy now," I said. "Don't try to talk until I tell you to. Save your strength." She started to nod and then her whole face wrinkled up as a new streak of pain shot through her body. I turned away for a minute; that kind of suffering was too hard to watch. Then the pressure of her nails diminished on my arms and I turned back to her. A moment of calm came into those slit like eyes. She tried to say something, but only garbled sounds came out. "Don't try to talk. Please. Not yet. You've got to tell me where to go, who is next. Biget must get through." She opened her mouth to speak again but I put my hand over it. "Don't talk until I tell you to. The big blonde." I said. "Is she on our side?"

The tiny eyes grew fearful. She shook her head. "Okay," I said, "she is not with us. Now, the ballet dancer, the one in the act, did he do this to you?"

She bit her lower lip and nodded.

"Did you tell him anything? Did you give him any information about Biget?"

I had to wait for the answer. A new series of pain was shooting through her. She held on hard to stay conscious. It would have been so much better to let her fall into a coma, or to have put a clean bullet through her and end the terrible suffering. When the pain had subsided a little she shook her head. "You told him nothing. That's good," I said.

"Now, tell me, who is next? Where do I go next? Who gets the message?" I put my ear close to her swollen lips. I could feel her lips move. I waited for the sound. She said four words. The first word and the last word were mumbled and I couldn't understand them. The other words were "world" and "Chloe." Something world, Chloe something. It was more than I expected. How she ever got that much out, I don't know.

Everything happened fast after that. I heard shuffling noises below. There were three men down there, the big fairy and two others. They were coming back for her. I should have known that they would. They had to get rid of the body. There was too much evidence on it, too many signs of the whip. If the body had been found it wouldn't have taken much to find the trail to the Chinese Keyhole. For a minute I wasn't sure what to do. If they took her alive, there was an outside chance they could shoot her full of some drugs and give her enough strength so that they could get the information they wanted. I couldn't let that happen. And if they took her alive, there is no telling how long she would stay alive, how many more hours of suffering she would have to endure.

She heard the noise of the fire escape being lowered and she knew what it meant. She could control herself no longer and she screamed. It was a great, loud, nerve-shattering screech, and then there was silence. There was an end to the scream and an end to the suffering. Her torn and beaten body squirmed no longer.

I had to move fast. This was no time to get caught. I sped out of the room and ran up to the third floor, looking for a place to hide. There were only three nameless doors again, leading to the apartments. I pushed one of the doors open, one that I thought was a front apartment. A figure came from somewhere. I let him have it and kept moving toward a window ahead of me. I looked down to the street below. It was a long jump and not a safe one. There was a small balcony below me. It was over the projecting front entrance of the building. Behind me I heard the sobbing voice of a woman saying a few Hail Marys. I took a deep breath, let myself down from the window ledge, and fell to the balcony. From there I jumped down to the ground and started running. I said a few Hail Marys myself. Mostly for the O.S.S., which taught a man how to jump and how to fall without killing himself.

When I came near a well-lighted cross street, I slowed down to a walk. It was a business thoroughfare with a streetcar line. I saw the single headlight of a streetcar a mile or so away. I stepped back into the dark doorway of a drugstore to wait for it. I caught my breath, straightened out my clothes, and combed my hair. I figured that outside of a couple of black and blue marks that might show up the next day, I had come out of it pretty clean.

I hopped on the almost empty streetcar and settled down in a seat, closing my eyes, pretending to sleep. I had a wisp of a thing to go on—something world and Chloe something. It wasn't much, it made no sense to me. It may have meant something to Biget, but I was under strict instructions not to try to contact headquarters.

The last "something" was probably Chloe's last name. I tried to think of any girl I knew whose name was Chloe. There had been one, but she was in France and it was a long time ago. The "something" that preceded "world" could have been anything. I tried fitting words together. They sounded fine but none of them meant anything.

The streetcar stopped. I sat up and opened my eyes. A very tired-looking tart got on, ignored all the empty seats, and sat down next to me. "Nice night, isn't it?"

"Is your name Chloe?"

She looked at me. "What are you, a wise guy or something?"

"I said is your name Chloe?"

"No. My name is Janice. My friends call me Jan."

"If your name isn't Chloe, get lost. Scram."

She got up and looked over at a sleeping drunk down the aisle. "Did you hear this guy? He's a real character."

I slumped down and closed my eyes again. This time I fell asleep. The next thing I knew was the conductor poking my shoulder. "It's the end of the line after the next stop, buddy. We go into the barn after that." I looked at my watch. It was ten to four. Another couple of hours and it would be time to get up and go to work. For some guys. Me, I still had my work to do.

When the car stopped, I got off and started walking down the street. I was whistling a tune and for a minute I didn't get the significance. The tune was "Chloe." That's who Chloe was, some dame in a song. It did me a lot of good. I thought about trying to find Jacques. It was against orders, but I thought maybe these circumstances were extenuating. I didn't know where to look for him. There was a saloon that he went to once in a while, but it closed up at two. Even if I had been able to find him, Jacques probably wouldn't have been any help. He had done his part of the job, he had given me the tie and given me the instructions. The rest was up to me.

My only hope was the big blonde. Maybe through her I could pick up some information that would make sense. I wasn't in the market for that kind of thing, but a job was a job. I was doing this one for my country. If it meant going to bed with an Amazon, what could I do?

CHAPTER FOUR

The big electric sign of the Chinese Keyhole was dark. I had no trouble finding the big blonde's apartment. The entrance to it was right next to the main entrance to the joint. I walked up a flight of stairs to the single door at the head of them. I had plenty of reservations about getting mixed up with her. She wasn't my type, for one thing, and there was danger of getting mixed up with her Chinese boyfriend or his pansy thug. But she was my only lead back to the clue the dead girl had given me. I had no other thread to follow.

Before I knocked at the door, I took off my shoulder holster and gun, hiding them in a dark corner of the landing. If I was going to play bedroom games with this girl, it would be a lot safer not to have the gun found on me. I double-checked to see if my knife were still in my pocket. It hadn't fallen out. I gave it a reassuring pat. I wasn't worried about that being on me. It looked like a scout knife. Nothing wrong with carrying a scout knife. It's an old American custom.

I was going on the assumption that the big blonde wasn't suspicious of me. I was going to play it straight. I was going to be John P. Maguire, struggling young lawyer, out for some kicks and laughs. I had to make her believe I was nothing more than a guy on the town. I wouldn't even let myself think about the possibility that she was smarter than I was playing her for, that she knew I was linked to the Chinese girl. If that were true, knocking on the door was like putting a gun to my head. I wouldn't have a chance.

But I had to have a chance. She was the only thing I had to go on. I straightened my tie, took a deep breath, and knocked. It was a little while before I heard any sound from inside. Then the door opened and she was standing there. Her blonde hair was mussed, her eyes full of sleep. She was wearing a man's flannel bathrobe, the old-fashioned kind, the kind my old man used to wear on Sundays. "Well, what do you know?" she said.

"What do you know, baby?"

"How come you decided to come back?"

"I got in the mood."

"You took a lot for granted, didn't you? How did you know I would still be in the mood?"

I shrugged my shoulders. "I took a chance, that's all. How about it?"

She stood aside. "Come on in. We'll talk about it." I followed her into the room.

It was a weird apartment. Some of the furniture looked as though it had been ordered straight out of the Sears, Roebuck catalogue; big, overstuffed, and upholstered in bright red. The rest of the furniture was Chinese, black and gold with a lot of gimmicks on it. "How about a drink, baby? I've got cotton in my mouth."

She ran her fingers through her hair. "You look like you've had a few too many as it is."

I shook my head. "Not enough. That's the trouble, I haven't had enough. Come on, get out the bottle and we'll drink a toast."

"To what?"

"To that stupid doorman of yours. Tell him when he goes after somebody, he shouldn't telegraph his punches. Surprise. Tell him that you've got to use the element of surprise."

She laughed as she poured two shots out of an unlabeled bottle. I didn't know what it was. It was almost clear, like gin. "He tried to tell me that you had a gang with you. I didn't believe him. I figured you were the kind who could take care of him alone."

"You ought to make him take a course in self-defense at the YMCA. It would do wonders for him."

"Is that where you learned?"

"I wouldn't know what to do without the YMCA." I took the shot glass from her. "What is this, vodka?"

"No, it's some Jap stuff. Very good, very potent. I save it for special occasions."

I held up the glass. "Here's to us, baby." I drank it down quickly. It tasted terrible, but once it was inside it felt good. She came over and stood in front of me. She was damn near as tall as I. In high heels she would have been right up there. It was a funny feeling. I'm used to bending down to grab stuff. But I didn't have to with her. I just leaned forward and there it was. Her mouth was open, her lips waiting.

Something had happened to me. Maybe it was the liquor she had given me, or maybe it was just that I had been through so much that night that I was susceptible to anything. But she didn't leave me so cold this time. I kissed her again and put a little heft behind it. She knew how to make a kiss count.

"You're all right," I said. My voice sounded thick. "You're all right." This time she kissed me. When it was over, I said, "I think maybe I ought to sit down."

"Do you think you can handle another drink?"

"Sure."

She started to walk away. "And handle me, too?"

I caught her arm and pulled her back to me and kissed her again. "Yeah, you too."

"I thought you had to sit down."

I smiled. "Go get the drink." I went over to the big red couch and sat down. There was a long, low Chinese table in front of it cluttered with a half-eaten box of candy, filled ash trays, and a slew of magazines and comic books. I pulled one of the magazines over, put my feet on top of it, and then leaned back. "You're very careful of the furniture," she said. "Your wife has you well trained. Does she make you do that at home?"

"Honey, I don't have a wife. I never had one, and if the saints are with me, I never will." I held up my hands. "Look, no strings."

She came over and gave me the drink. "You didn't look very married, but I thought I ought to find out."

"Would it have mattered?"

She shook her head. "I said that this was going to be for love, didn't I?"

I held up the glass. "For love." I swallowed it, making a mental note to put down twenty-five bucks on my expense account anyway. When the second drink had settled in my stomach, I was feeling no pain. It was hard to remember beyond the last time I had kissed her. "Come on down here," I said. "Put your head here."

She lay on the couch with her head in my lap. I leaned down to kiss her, fumbling with the belt of her bathrobe as I did. The robe fell open. It was a long stretch of beautiful skin, whiteness uninterrupted except for the taut brown peaks of her breasts and the glistening black pearl that was still in her navel.

"Is it real, baby?"

"What?"

"The pearl."

"Sure. It's a real Oriental pearl. Have you ever seen a black pearl this big before?"

"No."

"It's worth a fortune."

"Aren't you afraid some guy will pick it off you?"

"I'm careful," she said. "Very careful."

"How do you keep it there? Scotch tape?"

"A secret," she whispered. "It's a woman's secret."

I tried to pick the pearl out. The damn thing was stitched in there with surgical thread. She laughed at me. "Do you see now why I don't worry about it?"

"Doesn't it hurt?"

"It did at first, but it doesn't any more. I don't even know it's there."

I was getting hot under the collar. "Couldn't we go someplace more comfortable?"

She stood up. "Come in here. The equipment is better."

"What about Charlie? What if he shows up?"

"He won't show up."

"And lover boy? What about him? Maybe Charlie's got him playing watchdog."

She came back and sat down beside me again. "You worry too much." She took a peck at my ear. "I don't know what there is about you that gets me. Don't worry about anything. You won't get hurt any more than you want to."

"I'll take my chances with you, baby. It's the ballet dancer I'm worried about. I don't like the type."

She leaned forward and took a cigarette, lighting it quickly and snuffing out the match with her fingertips. "He's a rat," she said. "He's a damn pansy rat." She pulled down her robe and turned her back toward me. There were scars all over it, signs of the whip. "Someday I'm going to shoot that bastard. He gets his kicks with that whip. He's whip-happy."

"Why do you keep him around? Why don't you get rid of him?"

"Charlie won't let me. He does jobs for Charlie, some special stuff. Charlie likes the way he works. He likes him to keep an eye on me, too. He knows that Pete won't make a pass at me. Charlie's jealous as hell."

"If you were mine and another guy was trying to beat my time, I'd be jealous too."

"Yeah, but not the way he is. You don't understand what it means to him to sleep with a white woman."

"How did you ever get mixed up with him?"

She put the robe back over her shoulders. "How does anything happen to anybody? You get tired, I guess. You go through

45

the mill and you sink as low as you can, you can't sink no further. A guy comes and he's got dough, so you can relax, enjoy yourself. So he's not what a girl dreams about. So what? You don't know what it is to be hard up. You don't know what it is to crawl for a buck."

"Don't I?"

"It's different for a man. With a girl it's worse, you've got to take a lot. Sometimes you wish you didn't have a body. And I'm big, too big for most guys. It was always like that for me. I was always good enough for them to play around with, a change from the usual stuff. But they wound up marrying some sad-eyed little Susan, small and defenseless." She snorted a laugh. "Small and defenseless, hell. They think because I'm big, I'm different. I can take care of myself like a man, they think. Hell, you're no different. You're here for the novelty, I know that."

"If that's what you think, why do you want me?"

"I don't know. A change, maybe. Maybe just to get Charlie's goat. I don't know. Maybe it's because I like you in spite of anything."

"Does Charlie make so much dough from the Keyhole? He must make a lot of jack."

"He picks it up here and there. The Keyhole does all right. Charlie's smart. He knows people. But the hell with Charlie. Tonight it's us." She kissed me, then got up again and walked to the bedroom door.

I didn't want to go to bed with her, but I had to stick it out until I got a clue, a lead. I had got myself in so deep, I couldn't backtrack now, not without raising suspicions. This one was going to be strictly for Uncle Sam, strictly for security reasons. What a man does for his country!

She went on into the bedroom and I picked my feet up off the coffee table. As I did I noticed the magazine that had been under them. The name of the magazine was *United World*. It had a plain, scholarly-looking cover, very much out of place among the lurid, graphic covers of the other magazines and comic books. "What are you waiting for?" She was back at the door. I smiled and walked slowly toward her.

United World.

That had to be what the Chinese girl was trying to tell me. It made sense. *United World.* There was a reason for the magazine being in the blonde's apartment. Somehow, in some way, Chloe fitted into the picture. I was sure that by picking up the magazine and looking through it, I would discover the identity of Chloe. But I couldn't risk it now. I couldn't let the blonde see me looking at it.

I closed the bedroom door behind me. She was standing in the middle of the room. The bathrobe had fallen to her feet. And she was smiling at me.

The bedroom was also quite a room, bigger than the living room and a lot more elaborate. This room wasn't from Sears, Roebuck, this was strictly from Hollywood. It was all satin, lace, fringe, and thick carpeting you sank into a mile. There was the heavy, clinging musk of perfume. The bed must have been specially built. It would have slept six without any trouble. I had to shake my head a couple of times to make sure I was seeing straight. "Quite a layout you've got here."

"Like it?"

"Yeah, I like it fine." Suddenly I sensed that we were not alone. I looked around the room. Just in time to see a dog getting up from the thick rug.

It wasn't just an ordinary dog. Not with this tomato. She had to have a great Dane. And even for a great Dane it wasn't an ordinary dog; it was a damn big great Dane. He stood up and stretched his legs, looking at me distrustfully, snarling.

"Who's your friend, baby?"

"He won't bother you. His name is Hamlet."

Ninety per cent of all great Danes in the world must be named Hamlet. "That's cute," I said. "Very literary." The dog had walked over to me and was sniffing around. "How are you, Hamlet? What do you hear from Rosenkranz and Guildenstern?" The dog didn't think that was very funny. He let out a low growl.

The blonde snapped her fingers and the monster sauntered over to her and rubbed his side against her naked thigh. It looked like the beginning of an act you see at a stag. "Down," she said. "Go back and lie down."

The dog walked back to his corner, giving me a sniff and a snarl en route. "Is he going to stay here? Does he have to watch?"

"Don't be ridiculous," she said. "I'm going to the bathroom for a minute. Make yourself comfortable."

She closed the bathroom door and I decided to make a quick run back to the living room and check the magazine, to see if I could find the thread that would lead me to Chloe. But as I took one step toward the door, Hamlet growled and showed his teeth. I postponed the trip.

As I began to undress, I tried to remember what I knew about *United World*. It was a magazine put out by some people who were interested in forming a world government for peace. That made sense; it was a perfect vehicle for spreading information. The only thing I didn't know was who was using it, us or the other guys. I had a small debate on whether or not to take off my shoes, and I figured what the hell, I might as well enjoy myself. One thing I did do was to put my knife under one of the pillows. There was always that doubt about the lady, the possibility that she might not want me for my body alone. I was feeling pretty irresistible, but nonetheless I wasn't taking any chances.

I switched off the lights and lay on the bed. The sheets were silk. They felt wonderful against my body. I thought briefly that if I had to die in bed, I couldn't have picked a better one.

I heard the light switch click in the bathroom. The door opened and she came in. There was a growling sound suddenly from the dog. Then fast after that the window smashed. I heard the cracking sound of the whip following the shattering sound of the glass. I was on my feet. Lover boy was back. Maybe it wasn't the time and maybe it wasn't the place. I sure as hell wasn't dressed for it, but this was going to be my inning with the ballet dancer. I would have liked to see him pirouette his way out of this.

The blonde was scared. "Pete! Pete! Get out of here."

Pete's voice was soft. "Call off the dog or I'll kill him," he said.

"Get out of here, Pete. Leave us alone." The dog was really growling now and Pete was using the whip, because whining sounds were mixed with the barkings. I edged over to the chair and got my pants on.

"I'm warning you, Gail, I'll kill him."

"Stop it, Pete! Don't touch that dog." Then she called the great Dane. "Hamlet! Here, Hamlet!" She had the dog by the collar and started dragging him into the bathroom. She couldn't see me in the darkness, but she called out to me. "Watch out for him. He's got that whip. Make a run for it! Run!" She got the dog in the bathroom and locked the door.

Now there was not a sound in the room. I couldn't see him and he couldn't see me. "I'm not running, Pete. Come and get me. I'm waiting."

He answered with the lashing sound of the whip. I was barefoot and could move noiselessly over the thick rug. I called to him from different points of the room. Once, I was dangerously near the whip as he cracked it. I jumped up on the bed. The bedsprings squeaked and he spotted me. I turned my shoulders, but the whip came hard and cut deep. I jumped him before he got a chance to crack it again. I got him on the floor, pinned back the hand that held the whip, and twisted and twisted until he let go of it. I grabbed the whip and threw it out the broken window. "Okay, fancy pants, now we're evenly matched. How brave are you without the whip?"

It was with great pleasure that I sailed into him. It wasn't easy. He was tough. He was big and he was hard and he was a fighter.

How a guy like that got to be a queer, I'll never know. After he had landed a couple in my face, I figured maybe this queer stuff was an act with him. I didn't have time to analyze it thoroughly, because he followed through with a hell of a wallop to my belly. I felt all the beer I had been drinking make a big splash. The lights should have been on for that fight, because it was a good one. Tables fell over, lamps broke, fabrics tore. For a long time I didn't think I was going to be the winner. As a matter of fact, I wasn't the winner. It was a draw. We both got beat up bad. My hands were full of my own blood and his blood. He landed one lucky punch. It didn't knock me out, but I sailed across the room and fell against the wall, breathing hard, staying there for a minute until I got some strength back before I closed in on him with the knockout punch.

"I'll let up on you now," he said. His breathing wasn't so good either. "She won't want you bloody. You won't be any good for her until you heal up and get pretty again. If you're smart, bright boy, you'll stay away from her. You'll learn that when Charlie says something, he means it. Me, too. I mean what I say, too. Don't let it happen again, because the next time I won't be so easy on you."

I got Irish in me, I got a lot. And every last bit of it was up, fighting mad. Maybe I was going to wind up a dead Irishman, but I was going to finish off that guy or die trying to do it. But when I went for him he was gone, out through the window again. It wasn't over permanently. I swore to myself that I was going to get him if it was the last thing I did. After it was over, and I had done my job, no matter what, I was going to get that fancy phony and knock his pansy pants off.

When I flicked on the lights, I got a squint at myself in a broken mirror. I was really a mess. The only part of me that hurt badly was my arm where the whip had cut it. I found the kitchen and cleaned myself off, got the bleeding to stop, then I went back and finished dressing. I remembered to retrieve my knife from under the pillow. The blonde didn't come out of the bathroom.

On my way out I picked up the copy of *United World*. It didn't take me long to find what I was looking for. On the masthead, Chloe Renard was listed as associate editor. I put the magazine back under some comic books, went out into the hall, put my gun back in the holster, and then took off.

The guy in the song, the one who would go through dismal swamplands looking for Chloe, didn't have anything on me, not with what I had just gone through.

CHAPTER FIVE

There was an all-night lunchroom three blocks down from the blonde's apartment. They had a telephone book and the telephone book had a listing for Chloe Renard. I jotted down the address and telephone number. The joint was dirty but there was a smell of freshly made coffee. It was awfully tempting. But there wasn't time to dawdle. I walked till I found a taxi. Then I climbed in and gave the driver Miss Renard's address.

Daylight was just beginning under the darkness of the disappearing night. As we drove across town, the light became brighter. It was a little after five in the morning, a funny time of day. Everything was quiet and lifeless, without movement. The morning was an oil painting of city streets, it was an unidimensional backdrop in a vaudeville act. It was all there, all the color of the city, all of the dirt, and all of the splendor. It was there, but it seemed flat in the early-morning light, flat and without perspective.

The ride to Miss Renard's address was a long one. She lived in the university district. That meant something, too. There was a lot of hush-hush work still going on there and information leaking out. I had time, during the ride, for retrospection, to go back to the time Jacques had called me, review what had happened since then, and try to find a pattern for the events. The picture of myself sitting on the bed, thinking about Tina and thinking about love, didn't seem real now. It didn't seem that it could ever have been as important as I thought it was at the time. It was something that had happened weeks ago, it seemed. Weeks ago and to someone else. But I knew that when this was all over, it would happen again, I'd be faced again with living my own life. There was danger then, too. A different kind, more deadly because it didn't kill, it only tortured.

The events since midnight didn't have a pattern. They were many separate things laced together by an unknown binding. I wanted to know who that unknown binding was. It was somebody big and it was somebody important. As much as I wanted it to be, it wasn't really my job to find that out. Not yet, anyway. My job was a simple one of delivering a message. If Chloe Renard turned out to be the Chloe I was looking for, then my work would be done for the night.

In the song, Chloe must have been a plenty tasty dish. I had a feeling that I wasn't going to be so lucky with my Chloe. She was going to be the librarian type; high-collared, metal-rimmed spectacles, squeaky voice, an old maid withered on the vine. She would probably be just what I needed to get over the shock of the glamorous Gail.

I got to thinking about Tina again, wondering if she had expected me to come back to her place. Poor Tina. Tina took a lot from me. It was hard, sometimes, to keep from telling her that I was involved in espionage work. Sure, I horsed around now and then with a stray female who walked in front of me. I'm human and I'm not married to Tina. But I didn't play around nearly as often as Tina thought I did. Most of the time when she thought I was off with a girl someplace, I was doing a job. It was rough on both of us that I wasn't able to tell her about it. She went through nights of unnecessary anguish. It put me on the spot, too. What other excuse could I give than that I met a girl? You can only pull the sitting-up-with-a-sick-friend routine just so many times.

Women! I hoped Chloe Renard was eighty years old.

United World was a magazine devoted to spreading the gospel for world government. I knew that the movement for world government was getting a big build-up from the intellectual crowd. There were a lot of fancy people connected with it. And some not so fancy, just plain people. Every now and then there had been talk of Communist support and Communists working for the thing. I suppose there were. In a way, it was a natural medium for radicals. But I knew that the top people were solid, moneyed citizens. This meant that if anyone was using the magazine as a message carrier, it was most likely Uncle Sam.

That's what I knew about *United World* and world government. The rest I could learn from Miss Renard.

She lived in a big building, full of small apartments. I pressed the buzzer and in a few minutes the automatic signal opened the door. I took the elevator up to the seventh floor and looked for number 725. I knocked. The voice that answered was high-pitched and sleepy. "Who is it?"

"I want to talk to you, Miss Renard. It's important. Open the door, please." I kept my voice low. I didn't want to wake anybody else up.

"I can't open the door for you. I don't know who you are. What do you want?"

"This is urgent," I said. "I can't talk from out here."

"What's your name?"

"Maguire."

"I don't know you. I don't know anybody named Maguire."

"Sure you do. Think hard. My name is John B. Maguire. B. for Biget."

"Just a minute," she said. I waited for a couple of seconds. Then the knob turned. "All right," she said, "walk in."

Chloe Renard was quite a surprise to me. First of all, she was pointing a very dainty gun at me, rather unsteadily, but still a gun. And she was definitely not the librarian type. She was what we call in locker-room parlance the post college type; cute, well put together, plenty smart, hard to get, and harder to get rid of. Her hair was darkish blonde, curly and pulled up on the top of her head and tied with a ribbon, a blue ribbon yet. She was wearing what looked like an old-fashioned flannel nightgown. It had a high neck with some lace and ribbon around it, and it came all the way down to her bare feet. She was yawning. Yawning and pointing the gun at me at the same time.

"You want me to put my hands up?"

"You'd better," she said.

"Is that loaded?"

"I think so. I can't quite remember whether I loaded it or not."

"Well, maybe you ought to put it away."

"Identify yourself first."

She was cute, but I would have enjoyed her better if the gun had been someplace else. "What do you want me to say? I said Biget."

"How do I know that you didn't learn that from someone? How do I know you're really who you say you are?"

"You have to take that chance, honey." She studied me very intently for a minute and then put the gun down. "All right, I guess I'll take a chance with you." She opened the gun and said quite casually, "What do you know? It *is* loaded." She threw it on the couch. "Sit down while I go put something on."

"You've got enough on. All that shows is your feet, and I've seen bare feet before. As a matter of fact, you look very good for a woman getting up in the morning."

She gave me a sleepy smile. "I wish I could say the same for you. You look as if you had been through a meat grinder."

"I look better than this when I get up in the morning. You see, I haven't been to bed yet."

"What happened?"

"Well," I said, "that's a very long story. Can you make coffee?"

"There's some instant coffee in the kitchen. Go look while I wash my face."

The kitchen was in what is called apple-pie order. Everything was neat and clean, well arranged and trimmed uniformly in red and white checked edgings. Very homemakerish. I found the instant coffee and put some water on to boil. It would have to do.

When she came back she didn't look much different except that she was wearing fluffy blue slippers. "I'm a little more awake now. What do you want here?"

"Did you ever hear of me?"

"No. Was I supposed to? You do remind me of someone, though. At the moment I can't remember who." She thought a minute, then shook her head. "No, he was better-looking."

"Does the name C. Wong mean anything to you?"

Her blue eyes opened up and she looked frightened. "Charlotte?"

"Yes."

"What happened?"

I didn't say anything. The girl's lips formed the word "Dead," but no sound came out. I nodded my head. "That's it," I said.

She started to cry, just the way a baby cries. She screwed up her face and bit her lips and the tears started to come before there was a sound. Watching her, I wondered how a girl like that had got into this business. Everything about her, the way she looked, the way she had the apartment fixed up, indicated that she was cut out for the home life. She was ready-made to have a husband by the fireplace, pretty blonde children, and the country-club dances on Saturday night.

She was crying hard. I put my arms around her to steady her until she stopped. "I'm sorry," she said. "I know I'm not supposed to be like this. But just when you get to know someone and you begin to understand why they do what they do and you have respect for them and you think how wonderful they are to be so unselfish, something happens."

"Dry your eyes, baby. You're in a tough business." I heard the water boiling in the kitchen. I had to decide which was more important, to hold this girl or to drink a cup of coffee. With the way my luck was running, I decided on the coffee. In a couple of minutes she followed me into the kitchen.

"How did you find me, Maguire?"

"Because we're having breakfast together, you can call me John."

"How did you?"

"Charlotte told me before she died. She gave me your first name. I had to work the rest of it out for myself. Were you supposed to meet her?"

"I guess so. I mean, our deadline is today. I work on a magazine, and today all the copy goes to the printer, and she always gets the information to me by the time we're ready to send the stuff down."

That was one thing clarified. *United World* was on our side; we were using it. The editors of the magazine probably didn't know it, but we were using it. "How do you work in the stuff?"

"I have a column called 'One World.' It's little newsy items about world government, the kind of things women like to read. I get the messages from Charlotte, decode them, and recode them and work them into my column. It's a nifty way of doing it, don't you think?"

"Yeah, simply peachy. What happens after that?"

"I don't know exactly. Proofs of the magazine are airmailed out to our offices all over the world. In that way they can know what is going to be in ahead of time for promotions and things. I suppose the right people get the information."

"You say that the messages Charlotte gave you were coded?"

"Yes."

"Look at me."

"What on earth for?"

"Look at me." She looked now. "Do you see anything?"

"You have rather lovely eyes. Sort of like a cocker spaniel."

"I don't mean that. Keep your mind on your job." I grabbed my tie. "Look at this."

"Oh, that," she said. "I saw that ages ago. When you first came in. That's how I knew it was you. I mean that's how I knew you were who you said you were, because I recognized the code. I decoded it and wrote it down when I told you I was washing my face. It's not good."

"Tell me."

"Do you mind if I get some orange juice?"

"No, go ahead. You can get some for me."

She went into the refrigerator head first and came out with a milk bottle filled with orange juice in one hand, a carton of eggs in the other hand, and a package of bacon in her mouth. She closed the refrigerator with her fanny. It was a very cute performance.

"What does my tie say that's not good?"

She mumbled something through the bacon. I pulled the package out of her mouth. "What did you say?"

"I said that I don't think I should tell you. Here, hold this."

I looked at my hands, and they were full of a mixing bowl. "What are you going to do, bake a cake?"

"I'm going to scramble some eggs."

"For me too?"

"Certainly, for you too. Here, give it back to me. You're the nicest spy I've ever met."

"How many have you met?" I asked.

"Not many, really. I mean I may have met a lot without knowing what they were. But you don't look like a spy at all. You remind me more of a boy I used to know in Lincoln."

"Nebraska?"

"Certainly, Nebraska. Where else would Lincoln be?"

"I don't know. I never gave it much thought before. Are you from Nebraska, too?"

"No. Certainly not."

"Pardon me. I didn't mean to hurt your feelings. Where are you from?"

"Iowa," she said. She handed me a glass of orange juice. "Cedar Rapids. It's a frightful place to live. That's why I don't live there anymore."

"What do you think the folks in Cedar Rapids would say if a strange man took a shower in your apartment?"

"Heaven only knows. My grandmother would probably faint. You'll find towels in the cabinet in there."

"You're an angel." I leaned down and kissed the top of her head. This was more the size I was used to. As I started walking toward the bathroom she called me. "Maguire."

"What?"

"Just a minute." She went into a closet and came out a little self-consciously with a man's silk bathrobe. It was a beautiful robe. "This is—I mean this is my brother's. He stays here sometimes when he comes in from home. Cedar Rapids, that is."

I took the robe. "I'm willing to let it go at that. Thanks very much."

"Hurry up. The eggs will be done soon."

Besides getting a shower and using her brother's bathrobe, I borrowed a razor that was in the medicine cabinet and shaved. I felt pretty good. All I needed to feel human again was eight hours' sleep.

She had set the table in the kitchen. It was very pretty, very newly married looking. She laughed when she turned from the stove to look at me.

"What's so funny?" I said.

"The robe, it's so short. You look funny."

I looked down. The robe hit me this side of my knees. "The next time you get a brother, get one more my size."

The breakfast was good, the conversation even better. Neither of us talked about the Chinese girl or spies or Communists. I don't remember now what we did talk about. I remember I laughed a lot.

During the second cup of coffee, I got to thinking about these things again. On the surface my job was done. I had delivered the message and that was that. But the Chinese girl had told me that everything was about to break. Biget might not know that. I should tell them, I should get that information through. And I still had a score to settle with a sadistic ballet dancer. And the bubbling little girl on the other side of my coffee cup might be in danger. The magazine that I had seen in the blonde's apartment indicated that she and whoever else was with her knew that *United World* was being used to carry information. It was likely they knew Chloe was in it. I was concerned about her. It was hard to find somebody who scrambled eggs like that, just the way I liked them.

"What are you thinking about, Maguire?"

"Nothing. Nothing much."

"About Charlotte?"

I nodded. It was as good an answer as any.

"I was silly to cry. I wasn't surprised, really. I mean sometimes I realize how serious this thing is, the thing I'm doing. It's important to a lot of people all over the world. I think it's important to world peace. That's the reason I'm in it. One life doesn't matter when you think about the total effect of the work we're doing. Our life is so little to pay for thousands of lives that may be spared. I mean it could happen to me, even. Except that I'm not nearly so important as Charlotte was. She did lots of other things besides bringing me the information to send out. Important things. Were you able to talk to her for very long?"

"No," I said. "She was almost dead when I found her. There was very little time."

"Charlotte was terribly bright, really a fine mind. She understood about scientific things, knew what they meant. She was working to free her country. She thought that Communism would destroy any chance China might have for freedom. She wasn't blind to the other thing, either. I mean she knew that we had done badly in China, muffed the ball. But still she thought eventually it would be better. That's what she was devoting her life to. It makes me seem so infinitesimal."

"How long have you been at this?"

"Over a year. I don't think about it most of the time. Sometimes I forget that I'm doing anything out of the ordinary. I've had no contact with anyone but Charlotte before. I just went on living, forgetting most of the time that I was an honest-to-God agent. I mean, you know how girls are."

"No, how are girls?"

Her nose wrinkled up when she smiled. "Girls are always having crises. A man, usually. Or another girl having her hooks in your man. Things like that. Or they worry about hemlines, get terribly upset if they get shorter just after they've lengthened every dress they own. There are so many things every day, it's awfully hard to keep your mind on the important things."

"It sounds very rugged, being a girl."

"Well, that's just it, it isn't rugged. I do this work and it hardly means anything to me. I never realize really all the complications there can be. Then, suddenly, you show up and Charlotte is dead." She waited a moment, caught her breath. "Do you know who killed her?"

"No."

"How—how did it happen? What did they use? Was it a—" I opened my mouth but she put her fingers over it. "Don't tell me. Please don't tell me. I'd rather not know. I'm sorry I asked."

"I wasn't going to tell you, anyway."

"I dream a lot, and if I knew, I'd dream about it, I'm sure I would. I'd dream it was happening to me."

"How did you get in this? You're not the type."

Her face was quite serious. "Sure I am. I'm the type. It's a long story. Are you sure that you want to hear it?"

"Go ahead."

"The most important thing in the world to me is world peace. I loved a boy once, really loved him. I know that I'm no different from any other girl who lost a man in the war. I mean, I didn't feel it any more than anyone else. I'm trying to say that it hurt everyone it happened to, not only me. But I was mad, too. I was mad because I was cheated out of him. He was wonderful. He had a great big smile and he was going places. I was mad when he wasn't there anymore. Mad enough to want to fight for peace. That's how I became mixed up in world government. It made sense to me, it seemed to be the beginning or a way of beginning peace. Am I sounding awfully maudlin?"

"No. You're sounding like a girl, a very sensible girl. And very pretty."

"Well, that's all there is, really. I mean, I came here to work for the magazine and I was approached about this other thing. It was another way to fight."

"What about him, the boy who was killed? Did you ever get over him?"

"Yes. Maybe it's a pretty cruel thing to say, but I did get over him. I got older, my perspective changed. I could only remember him the way he was when I saw him last. After a while of remembering him, he seemed so young to me, so impractical. I suppose if I could have made him grow older in my remembering, I wouldn't have got over him. I mean, if he had lived he would have developed and matured. We'd have grown older together. This way it was only I who grew older, and as I grew older I stopped hanging onto my memories of him. Does that sound garbled and female to you?"

"It makes sense, I guess. Some of it."

"What happened was that I started out working because I was mad, but as the anger disappeared there was something else to take its place, to make me want to continue to work. I understood things, I had some intelligence about them."

"You're a nice girl," I said. "I haven't known many like you."

"Thank you. I'm glad you like me. I happen to be a divine cook, too."

"I can tell."

"No, I can really cook. I make the loveliest soufflés. I know every girl thinks she can make soufflés, but mine are really divine."

It was inevitable that I should compare her to Tina. I was thinking this was the girl that Tina would like to be. She knew all the things that Tina never had time to learn. Tina was like me: What she got, she fought for. There wasn't time in her life to learn about soufflés or how to put shelf paper in the kitchen. I was thinking that maybe Tina was right, maybe this kind of girl was what I wanted. Maybe all the chases after the wild females were for nothing. Maybe this was the unknown thing that I seemed to be continuously seeking. At that moment, it was the answer, it was everything I wanted. But I couldn't be sure. There had been other moments with other kinds of girls when I had felt the same way. And those moments had come to nothing. And so might this.

"You're a funny man, Maguire. You're very pretty, too. A little scarred at the moment, but very pretty. You have the longest eyelashes. I've been watching them."

"I'm not in your league, little one. There's a big difference between you and me. You're in this racket because you're fighting for an idea. I'm in it because I can't make a living any other way. Dough. I struggle for it all the time, and there isn't any time left over to think about deep, fundamental things."

"I don't believe you. I don't believe what you say is true. You may tell yourself that, you may try to believe it, but I bet you don't. I bet you've got a great big fat soul somewhere. And a conscience. I don't think you're nearly as tough as you want me to think." She punctuated the sentence with a crinkled-nose smile. A little more of that technique and she could have made me believe anything.

The doorbell rang. She jumped. "Who do you suppose that could be?"

"I don't know. Find out. Can you talk to them downstairs?"

"Yes." She went over to the instrument on the wall and pushed a button. "Who is it?"

A voice came up. "Western Union." She looked at me. I nodded. She pressed the buzzer. "Do you suppose it really is Western Union?"

"I don't know. We'll find out." I drew my gun and stood behind the door when she opened it. Through the crack I could see a regular uniformed messenger boy. She took the telegram and signed for it. I put my gun away. "False alarm," I said.

She opened the telegram and her face was concerned. She went to the desk, took a pencil, and began writing on the yellow paper, referring to a small black book that she took from her drawer. I looked over her shoulder. The telegram was from Cedar Rapids:

HAVE NOT HEARD FROM YOU IN TWO WEEKS. ARE YOU ALL RIGHT? PLEASE WRITE AT ONCE. WE HAVE BEEN CONCERNED.

GRANDMOTHER

"From Biget?" I asked.

"I guess so. They said that they might sometime if it were important. They haven't, though, until now." She continued to work words back and forth from the telegram to the code book. "Oh, golly," she said.

"What's the matter?"

"It says I'm in danger. Polyton knows. Proceed with extreme caution." She chewed the end of the pencil. "What do I do now?"

"Who's Polyton?"

"He's such a nice little man. He works on the magazine. He doesn't do much. He used to be a professor or something, but he got too old and they retired him. He does our copy editing for us. I'm sure there must be some mistake."

"Biget doesn't often make mistakes."

"Yes. I suppose you're right. But it seems so silly. He just sits there all day. He looks so meek and mild. He wouldn't hurt a fly."

"Would it be possible that he is getting information out through the magazine, too?"

"I suppose he could. He changes copy once in a while, makes corrections and things. You mean you think that both sides are using it?"

"It's possible. It may be that Polyton is just a contact man. If he's been around the university for a long time, it's very likely he can get a lot of information. Particularly if he has the reputation of being a nice man who wouldn't hurt a fly."

"You just can't trust anyone, can you? He's always been so nice to me. He's the first one I would have gone to if I had been in trouble of any kind."

"Are you scared?"

"I don't know. I suppose I am. I mean, wouldn't you be if you didn't know who your friends were and they told you to proceed with extreme caution?"

"Sure I would. I'm scared now."

"What have you got to be afraid of?"

"I'm afraid something will happen to you."

She looked down at the floor, tracing a circle with her fluffy blue slipper. "That's very nice of you, Maguire. To be worried about me, I mean." Then she looked up. "I'll be all right, though."

"What are you going to do?"

"Nothing, except what I always do. I think that's the best way, just to pretend I don't know anything about anything. I'll get the message through today as I always do. Gee, sometimes I think maybe it would have been better if I had married that boy from Lincoln."

"Nebraska?"

She laughed. "Sure, Nebraska. There's nothing wrong with Nebraska."

"Look here, I've got to get moving. I have a feeling I'm going to have work to do."

"Go in the bedroom and get dressed. I'll clean up in the kitchen."

When I came out, dressed and ready to go, she was in the kitchen looking very thoughtful as she dried the dishes. "I'm ready to go," I said.

She dried a little faster. "Well, good-by."

"Is that all? Aren't you glad we met or anything?" "Yes, I'm very glad, Maguire. I'm very glad we met." She put down the dish and held out her hand for me to shake. I ignored the hand and took her into my arms and kissed her softly. When I let go she threw her head back and said, "Now I *am* scared. You kissed me as though you were never going to see me again."

"I won't be seeing you again, Chloe. Not because I don't want to, and it's not because I think anything is going to happen to you. It's against regulations, remember? We're not supposed to be together even now. You know how important it is to keep your identity a secret. They know about you. I can't take the chance of being seen with you, of arousing suspicion. I'd lose my effectiveness. I'd be a dead duck for sure."

"I don't think it's fair for you to disappear out of my life when you've only just come into it. I could disguise myself or something and then we could meet. I played a scrub woman once in a show in college. Everyone said that if they hadn't known it, they wouldn't have believed it was I. I mean if I were in real trouble and I thought of a way to disguise myself, where could I find you?"

"Don't try it. It's not safe. Really, it isn't. Only if you're desperate, really desperate." I gave her my address downtown and at home and my telephone numbers. "Don't worry, Biget will look after you. And in my own way, I'll look out for you, too. I'll keep nosing around to see that you're safe and sound. But promise me something."

"What?"

"If you ever see me on the street or in a crowd or anywhere, don't recognize me. Forget that you ever knew me. Forget that I borrowed your brother's bathrobe and ate breakfast across from you."

"Maguire?"

"What?"

"I've got something to tell you."

"About the bathrobe?"

She nodded.

"I don't want to hear," I said.

"You're very sweet, Maguire." She came up to me, stood on her tiptoes, and kissed me. "Now, go away fast and maybe I can forget you were ever here."

I took her in my arms, just holding her. "Take care," I whispered, "take care."

"The bathrobe," she whispered, "it really does belong to my brother."

CHAPTER SIX

More pieces of the puzzle were fitting together. *United World* was an unimportant part of the United States espionage system, I knew that. It was a minor-league operation, a slow means of spreading information to overseas agents. There had to be another reason for having Chloe there, a reason that probably even she didn't know. One of the big leaks in scientific data was from the university. Maybe they had put Chloe there to observe. Maybe this Polyton was the brains of the spy ring. There were many possibilities. If I could only get the go-ahead to track it down, to follow through. I wanted that more than anything.

There was no point in going back to my apartment, so I went directly to my office. Rather, I went first to Tina's office, which was on the floor below mine. Tina was at her typewriter in the back, near the window, working. The girl who worked for her was busy on the telephone. She smiled and waved to me when I came in. Tina didn't look up. Together these girls were the answer to a struggling lawyer's dream. They were his telephone service, stenographic service, and love counselor, and in a pinch you could get one of them to loan you five for a few days.

I went over to Tina and coughed a couple of times before she looked up. She looked up and then down at her copy again. "You look swell, Counselor. You're the kind of man I always wanted. I used to dream about a man with red eyes."

"Bloodshot?"

"Still bleeding."

I rubbed my hands over my eyes. "It was a rough night," I said.

"I betcha. She must bite and have long fingernails. Anybody I know, darling?"

"No. As a matter of fact, I'm pretty sure it's no one you know, unless you've been palsy with a new crowd lately. I'm sorry I didn't get through soon enough."

"I kept a light on in the window for you, foolish girl that I am. All I drew were three moths and a mosquito."

"Do you have to keep typing when I'm talking to you?"

She hadn't missed a beat on that damn machine. "Darling, you're beautiful and I love you. Bloodshot eyes and all, I love you. But you are not what a girl considers the steady type. This typewriter is. If I don't want to wind up in a home for destitute middle-aged ladies, I have to remember that L. C. Smith is my very best friend."

"Try warming your feet against it on a cold night," I said.

"It has its disadvantages, Johnny. But then, so do you."

I sat down, lighted a cigarette, and put it between her lips; then I lighted one for myself. "Damn it, you could take two minutes off to be nice to me. I need a cool hand on a ruffled brow. I need someone who understands me."

"Try a psychiatrist. I'm not feeling very understanding this morning."

"Aw, come on, Tina, stop typing for two minutes."

She stopped, stood up, and started to walk away.

"Now, where are you going?"

"Not far," she said. She went far enough to get a Bromo-Seltzer.

"I don't need that. I'm not hung over."

She went right ahead and mixed it up until it was a frothing, nauseating-looking mess. "Drink it, Counselor."

"I tell you that isn't my trouble. I'm not hung over."

"Darling, your eyes tell me different."

Instead of arguing, I drank it. It tasted terrible.

"And now that you've taken your medicine like a good boy, I have a present for you." She pulled two ties out of her desk drawer.

"Where did you get these?"

"That isn't polite. Even if you don't like them, you're supposed to say that they're very pretty and you're supposed to thank the nice lady who gave them to you."

"Thank you. They're very pretty," I said. "Now, for Christ's sake tell me where you got them."

"A divine-looking Frenchman sold them to me. He's sort of the Charles Boyer type. A little more hair, perhaps. He's been peddling them all over the building this morning. All hand-painted in France, no two alike."

I grabbed the ties and kissed Tina lightly on the cheek. "They're beautiful and you're divine. Good-by."

"But Johnny..." I kept walking. I had to find Jacques in a hurry.

I left the door to my office open and waited. In about ten minutes Jacques poked his head in. "Would monsieur like to see some beautiful hand-painted neckwear from France? Very beautiful, very inexpensive."

"I've got nothing but time. Bring them in." Jacques and his suitcase came in. He opened the thing and spilled some ties on my desk. "What's up, Jacques?"

"It did not go so well last night, yes? Trouble?"

"Plenty of trouble. I've got to see Biget. Right away. I've got a fistful of information to be delivered."

"Did you find out who killed Tom?"

"No. I could if I got the chance. I've got all the leads I need."

"This place, Johnny, this Chinese Keyhole, you found there something?"

"I don't know, Jacques. I've found a lot of things."

"You think maybe you can solve the whole thing, find the head of the organization?"

"I've got a good chance."

"You want me to do anything, Johnny? Follow any leads?"

"I can't give orders like that, Jacques. You know it's against regulations."

"I thought on my own time…"

"Thanks, Frenchie. I know you're trying to help, but I've got to get the assignment first. I've got to have carte blanche to crack this thing. You've got to get me in touch with Biget right away."

Jacques smiled. "It is arranged."

"What do you mean?"

"I have the news for you. Biget wants to see you. I was given the message early this morning. I have the instructions."

"Who is he?"

"I don't know who he is. Biget. That's all I know."

"That is all I know, too. Biget could be anyone."

"You don't contact him directly?"

"No. I have never seen him. It is another carrier who brings the instructions to me."

"Biget must have two heads or something. Nobody ever sees him. Somebody must know who he is."

"You will, Johnny. At eleven-fifteen today."

"What are the instructions?"

Jacques took a key from his pocket. It was a hotel key. He threw it to me. It was from the Stevens Hotel. It was the key for Room 1702. "You are to go there and wait."

"Is that all?"

"Yes, that is all."

"You don't know what he looks like or anything?"

Jacques shook his head and began to gather up the ties. "How about it, Johnny, maybe you want to buy a tie from France? Very beautiful."

"That's some racket you've got with those ties. The government buys them as props for you and you sell them and pocket the dough. Quite a racket."

"It is not a racket, Johnny. I do not sell any." He picked up a particularly hideous-looking specimen. "Who would buy these terrible things?"

"You're a liar, Frenchie. You're a damn liar. You sell them and pocket the dough. I know. My girl bought two of them for me as a present."

Jacques smiled a little sheepishly and shrugged his shoulders. "She is very pretty."

"I know she's very pretty, but you took her for a ride." I took the ties out of my pocket and threw them in with the rest. "Come on, sharpie, kick back."

"Kick back? What is it, this kick back?"

"Don't play dumb. I've known you too long. The dough, give it back." I held out my hand and he finally got around to putting four dollars into it. "Listen, Jacques, if I find out that she paid more than two bucks apiece for these, I'll take the difference out of your hide."

"No, wait." He pulled another dollar out of his pocket and gave it to me. He was smiling. "One must try," he said. "One must always try."

As soon as Jacques left, I went to my apartment. There was time before my scheduled meeting with Biget to change clothes and catch a little shut-eye. I peeled off my clothes and fell on the bed, expecting to doze off the minute I felt the pillow. But I guess that I was overtired, too stimulated to fall asleep quickly. There was a lot to think about. I had been curious about Biget for a long time, ever since I had been working on this information leak to China. I was a little excited about meeting him, I guess. The guy, if he was a guy, was imaginative, had a feel for this business. I could tell from my instructions and missions. He seldom made a suggestion, but when he did, it paid off. I knew this much, that something important, really important, was going to happen if a direct meeting had been arranged. It was very unusual.

There was time to think about the little girl with the ribbon in her hair. My eyes were closed, but I could see the way she had looked in the kitchen, puttering around. It was a novelty for me to be thinking about a girl any place except in a bedroom. It was fun for a change. I was wondering how long it would last, if things had been different and I could have seen her again. I was wondering how many years it would take until I would be tired of watching her make breakfast. Maybe it wouldn't take years. Maybe it would only take a couple of weeks until I was bored to death with that cute homemaker routine. Then again, maybe I'd never get tired of it. That kind of thing is hard to tell.

I was hoping she would stay out of trouble. I was beginning to have a yen for soufflés. I was at the soufflé point when I finally fell asleep. I hadn't been asleep long when the alarm went off. It was time to get ready.

At eleven-fifteen promptly I was opening the door to Room 1702 of the Stevens Hotel. The room was empty. It looked pretty much as all six-dollar-a-day hotel rooms look. No better, no worse. I checked the room for concealed wiring. It was as clean as a whistle. So were the drawers and closets. I flopped on the bed and leafed through the Bible that was on the stand next to it. There was a telephone number scribbled alongside the Twenty-third Psalm. It probably didn't mean anything, but I remembered it just in case.

Eleven-thirty went by and there was still no action. By twelve o'clock I was getting a little jumpy. Then I heard the sound of a key in the lock. My hand went on my gun. Then a pause. Very quickly the door opened and a man came in, closing the door. His back was to me. I had my gun out.

"Biget," the man said.

"Biget."

He turned around and I had to look twice before I was sure. "Colonel Jenkins!" I jumped to my feet and came to attention.

Jenkins said, "At ease, for Christ's sake. You're out of the Army, remember?"

They trained me well in the Army. I was responding as readily as a trick dog in a vaudeville act. "How are you, sir?" I said. "I'm glad to see you."

"I'm fine, Maguire. I see you haven't changed any." He was pointing to the dent in the bed where I had been resting. "Still horizontal most of the time?"

"Whenever possible, Colonel."

"Drop the Colonel, will you? I'm Sam Webb from Day-ton, Ohio."

"I'm really glad to see you," I said. "I didn't know what had happened to you. I was never sure. I tried to find out, but no one ever knew. Do you remember the last time we saw each other?"

"There isn't time for reminiscing, Maguire. It's something I don't indulge in." He sat down and lighted his pipe. "There's a big job to do. I want to know if you think you can handle it."

I sat on the bed and waited for him to tell me about it. Jenkins was a man I owed my life to. It was as simple as that. If it hadn't been for him, I would be dead. He got me out of an impossible situation, risked his own neck doing it. It was in Germany toward the end of the war. I was doing a job with a German underground outfit. One of them ratted on the operation and we were taken prisoners. The Germans were executed immediately, but they held me to have some fun with. I was kept in a cellar of a house. Four crack Nazi officers, armed with bayonets, showed up one night slightly drunk. They backed me against a wall and took turns jabbing at me, just missing me, sometimes grazing me slightly. There was nothing I could do. Every time I lunged for them, they beat me up a little. They were playing with me the way a cat plays with a mouse.

They showed me the execution orders. I was a dead pigeon anyway, but a firing squad would have been a cleaner way to die.

One of the officers explained that it might be necessary to retreat before morning, so I was to die that night.

Against his own orders, for one man's life was not important compared to a total job, Colonel Jenkins showed up, springing from nowhere, and sprayed machine-gun fire into the cellar. The Germans were taken by surprise, but they still had time to get off a couple of shots. One of them got me in the arm. I started running, and as I ran down the street I could still hear the sound of the machine-gun fire in that basement. Jenkins got out; that much I knew, because I saw him leave the building running in the opposite direction from me.

I never saw him after that until now. I could never contact him or reach him in any way. I had never had a chance to thank him. I did now.

"For what?"

"For that cellar in Rothsgart."

He smiled quickly. "Shut up about it. It was against orders. Don't think I'll always be there to do it."

"How did you know where they were keeping me?"

"Do you remember a girl named Marga Mueller?"

I guess maybe I blushed. I did remember her, vividly.

"Yes, I think I do."

"You know damn well you do, Maguire. I had her after you. It's not a thing you forget so quick. She told me. She knew where you were."

"I guess I ought to look her up some time and thank her."

"I've got something more important if you want it, Maguire."

"Are you kidding? You damn well know I want it. For a lot of reasons. Go ahead, what's the deal?"

"I think you'd better start. What happened last night? We've lost contact with one of our agents."

"The Chinese girl?"

"Yes."

"She's dead," I told him. "She was beaten to death with a whip. Unmercifully. She was nothing but raw, tortured flesh when I found her. She was just alive enough to whisper the clue leading to the next in line for the message. Hey, what about that, anyway? What was the idea of sending me out with that message? I thought maybe it was going to be something big. I wound up with a jane named Chloe who codes stuff for a magazine."

"Yes, I know."

"Isn't that stooge work? This *United World* can't be a very important operation for us."

"It's not in itself. We use it for routine transmissions. But it's a good place to have an agent planted. You must realize by now that the university is a hot spot for spies. This girl doesn't know it, but she's doing a big job for us. She has instructions to watch everything that goes on around her. She may be of great help."

I ran my finger around my collar. "Maybe so," I said.

"What else about last night?"

"They're never going to find the Chinese girl's body. The guy who did the whipping job came back to get her. Her body was full of evidence. The whip lashes. I know who did it. It would give me great pleasure to—"

"That isn't important now. Listen, Maguire, what you did last night, delivering an unimportant message, may have seemed trivial to you. It wasn't. This thing is getting to a point where we have to stop it before it's too late. Every single movement of that spy ring is important. Any simple event may turn out to be not so simple; it may turn out to be the opportunity we've been waiting for, to crack this ring, to crack it at its source. I know you, Maguire. I know your capabilities. I wouldn't waste them on anything that didn't require your special brand of talent. Everything has importance now, every assignment."

I hesitated a minute. It was going to be hard to say. "The night before last—do you know about that?"

"You were given an assignment. It was carried out. What about it?"

"I didn't carry it out. I didn't go. I didn't think it was important. I sent my assistant, Tom White, only..."

"Only what?"

"Something must have happened after he did the job. He was killed. Didn't you know?"

"No. I didn't know. I knew that what was supposed to be done was done. I didn't know anything happened after that."

"Tom must have run into something. It must have been big; otherwise they wouldn't have killed him. He must have stumbled across a lead. If I hadn't been such a lazy, self-centered sonofabitch, I would have gone myself. I should have known that you wouldn't be wasting me on carrier-pigeon stuff. But I didn't know. If I had gone, I'd have the lead Tom ran across. I'd have the key to this whole spy works right now. And," I added, "Tom would be alive."

"A man can make a mistake, Maguire. You made an error in judgment. Maybe it was my mistake. We let you hire Tom White to do legwork for you, so you would be free to carry the ball when the time came. I should have specified in my orders that you were to do the job. It's done with now, Johnny. It's over. You can't bring your pal back to life and you can't retrace and pick up the lead he found. You'll have to start over, find it yourself."

"You still want me to do it—the big job, I mean?"

"Sure. Now finish telling me about last night."

I told him the whole story, start to finish, from the Chinese Keyhole to Chloe. He listened carefully but his mind was working all the time, putting pieces of the puzzle together.

When I finished he said, "That goes together with some things we already know. It explains a lot more. It works this way: there are many experiments being carried on in this area with atomic power. There are weapons being tested and developed that are unbelievable. Some of the work is in harnessing atomic power to run industrial machinery. It's the kind of information that a lot of countries would like to get hold of. There are three universities around here where these experiments and research are being carried out."

"I thought there were only two," I said. I named them. "What's the third?"

"Midwestern Tech."

"It's such a small school. A funny spot to be running something so big."

"That's the reason. Because the job is so big, a small inconspicuous school was picked as one of three. But there's a man here in the city named Polyton. We discovered last night that he is the final source for this information. He's the one who collects it from all three schools and passes it on to the head man of the spy organization. We're not sure if he passes it directly or if it goes through another hand before it gets to the big brains. We know the workers in each lab who are smuggling the information out. We've known them for some time. As a matter of fact, you've spotted several for us."

"Five," I said. "I kept count."

"We let them alone. They're still not touched. We let them alone because we knew that we'd catch the control man that way, that one of the workers would eventually lead us to him. Your friend Chloe put the finger on Polyton for us, without knowing it. You see, someone got wise to Chloe and showed his hand by intercepting Chloe's messages. That's how we found out who it was. It was this man Polyton. He works in her office in some kind of advisory capacity for the magazine. No one on the magazine suspects him of being anything more than he appears: a nice old retired professor."

"Chloe knows," I said. "She was warned."

"I made sure she was warned," Jenkins said.

"Tell me one thing," I said. "I won't ask any more."

"What is it?"

"This girl Chloe. How much danger is she really in?"

"What's the matter, Maguire, have you fallen for her already?"

"I just want to know."

He smiled. "I wish I had the strength of your back."

"It isn't anything like that. She just seems out of place in all this. Defenseless."

"That's why we hired her, because she *does* look like that. Don't underestimate her, Maguire. She's a smart cookie, a very smart one. To tell you the truth, I don't know how much danger she really is in. If they think all she's doing there is coding messages through the magazine, they'll leave her alone. They'll realize that what she's putting through is minor stuff. However, if they suspect that she knows more than that, if they think she's been planted there to watch anyone, I wouldn't give you a plugged nickel for her life. I know this much, Maguire: if I were running the spy ring, I wouldn't take a chance. The girl is in a position to know too much. I wouldn't take the chance of letting her tell it to anyone. Maybe they're not that smart. For her sake, I hope they're not."

"Okay, that's what I wanted to know. Now, what else about this spy organization?"

"All information gets into Polyton's hands. A couple of times it's been more than information. Pieces of machinery have been stolen. Whatever it is, it gets to Polyton. He passes it on to someone, somewhere. That's the top of the organization. The information is put together, combined with other information, cooled, and sent to another branch of the organization, which gets it out of this country and into China."

"The organization that gets it out of the country sounds like the bunch at the Chinese Keyhole."

"It must be," Jenkins said. "We knew that the Keyhole was linked in some way. That's why we put the Chinese girl there. She must have had a lot more to tell than you heard. She must have learned something very important."

"It makes sense, though, that the Keyhole would be the organization to get the information out. I noticed they have a souvenir department with a lot of imported stuff. They must have direct traffic with China. Lots of opportunities."

"The blonde strip artist and her Chinese boyfriend must contact the key man. Polyton also contacts him, directly or indirectly. As you know, Maguire, even if we get evidence against them, it won't do any good. Nabbing Polyton or the gang at the Keyhole would only set us back. The key man would find another setup, another bunch of traitors, and we'd have to start all over again to find him. Maybe it isn't a him, maybe it's a woman. Your job is to find that key person. Get him and the rest of it will collapse. The whole spy ring will fall apart when we remove the key man."

"What about Charlie Moy?" I asked. "The blonde's boyfriend? Is it possible that he's the brains of this?"

"I don't think so. He's the head of the bunch at the Keyhole, but he isn't the big man."

"There are no other leads?"

"You know as much as I know, Maguire. The rest is up to you."

"You don't care how I go about this?"

"No, you go ahead and do it your own way. But I think the blonde sounds like your best bet right now. She sounds dissatisfied with the setup there. Play up to her. Maybe she'll talk a little."

"What about breaking regulations?"

Jenkins thought a minute. "You mean the girl from Iowa?"

"Yes."

"I think that that's almost necessary. She may have the answer for you, Maguire. She was put at *United World* to be able to answer questions when the time came. The time has come. If you take what she knows and put it together with what you know, maybe you'll have the answer. But be careful. Don't let anyone see you with her. They know about her. If they see you with her, they'll know about you too, and neither of you will be worth a damn to us."

"I'll be careful," I said. "So far I'm in the clear. The blonde isn't suspicious of me. She thinks I'm just a guy on the make. Charlie and his whip artist don't like me, but I don't think they're suspicious. I'll get the man, Colonel Jenkins. Don't worry about that. I'll get him."

He gave me a telephone number to memorize. "Don't phone until you have the complete information. Don't phone me to give me pieces of information or to ask questions. It's too risky. Phone me when you've got him—or her, or whoever it is."

"When I find him, what do you want me to do—kill him or bring the bastard in alive?"

"I don't want to sound corny, Maguire. You should know this, you should have picked it up someplace in your law training. Everyone in this country is entitled to a fair trial. It's in the Constitution. We'd be working a lot faster if we could just trigger the persons we know are foreign agents or traitors. But in this country you can't touch them until you have proof, and you can't jail them or execute them until they have stood trial and have been proved guilty. You've got to try to get evidence, Maguire. It's not going to be enough to get the man you're after without evidence. We all may know he's guilty, but it has to hold up in court. You know that." Jenkins stood up. "You were asking about bringing him in dead or alive. Try to bring him in alive, but don't forget the evidence. However, if the sonofabitch gives you a bad time and you've got to pull a gun on him to save your own neck, that's something else."

"Okay. That's what I wanted to know."

Jenkins smiled. "You're angry now, Johnny. You're mad at the guy because he killed your buddy. You're mad at all of them because they have killed good people, people who are working for the security of their country. But when the showdown comes, you'll remember who you are, you'll remember about basic principles of democracies. You won't shoot them down in cold blood. You hate them too much to use their methods. I'm not worried about that, Johnny. You'll bring him in the right way."

"Could be," I said. "You could be right. But I hope he gives me a bad time. I hope I have to use self-defense."

"You stay here in the hotel room for ten minutes after I leave. Then take the key, lock the door, and drop the key in a mailbox down the street." He held out his hand. "Good luck, Maguire."

I waited ten minutes after he had gone, then I tore out of there.

CHAPTER SEVEN

The afternoon was filled with sunshine, the streets active with people going about their business. I had my job to do now. This was it. This was the big thing. No more frustrating regulations; the field was clear for me to do as I thought best.

Jenkins had suggested contacting the big blonde. She was strictly a nighttime girl. I would have to wait until later. Chloe seemed my best bet. I felt that if we pooled our information, I could come up with the answer. But it was too early for Chloe to be home from work. I didn't want to risk contacting her at her office. Meanwhile, I thought it would be a good idea to find what I could about Charlie Moy. I called a friend of mine at the city hall, who looked up the record on the liquor license of the Chinese Keyhole. There were three owners listed: Charles Moy, Ruth Moy, and Gail Nevaire. Ruth Moy was a new name to me. I figured maybe it was Charlie's wife, but her home address was different from his. I memorized that address just in case.

Going to Moy's house was playing a hunch. I wasn't looking for anything in particular. I was looking for a hint, a clue, a straw to grasp. Moy was in contact with the big boss. Somewhere, somehow, I was sure that there would be something among Moy's possessions that would give me the lead.

The house was a big one, in a part of town that had been a good neighborhood fifty years before. Now Moy's place stood in well-kept contrast to the dilapidated mansions-turned-rooming-houses adjoining it. I stood on the opposite side of the street counting windows in the place. There were going to be a lot of rooms to search.

I got into the house through a basement window. It smelled worse down there than any basement I had been in recently, more damp and more rancid. I listened for some sound above me. There was none. It wasn't reasonable that the house would be empty. There would have to be servants around, but I heard no footsteps. Then I realized that maybe Moy had the soft-shoe kind of Chinese servant. I couldn't have heard one of those birds if he had been walking behind me.

But two can play that shoeless game. I took off my size twelves, tucked them under my arm, and started up the back stairway. I landed in the kitchen. It was empty. It was more than empty. It hadn't been used in a long time. Dust was coated heavily over all the antiquated appliances; cobwebs linked the corners of the ceiling. There was a steady drip from the faucet in the sink in the butler's pantry. It was an old leak; there were rust marks where it hit the drain.

Two doors led out of the kitchen, one of them obviously to the dining room and the other, I figured, into the hall. I played eeny-meeny to decide which one would squeak the least when I opened it. I lost. The door to the hall made one hell of a squeak, and besides that, it was the swinging kind; it kept swinging and squeaking. I froze motionless and waited for someone to show up and see what the racket was about.

Nobody showed.

As I walked down the hall, looking in room after room, I realized that they would all be the same. The house hadn't been lived in for at least ten years. Everything was loaded with dust and laced with cobwebs. The furniture was the most fantastic I've ever seen, ornately carved teak-wood, lots of gold with grotesque carvings ornamenting it. It didn't add up. The outside of the house was in good shape; the lawn was mowed and the hedges were trimmed. The front door had been recently painted. And inside it was like this.

Upstairs it was the same thing. There were a couple of kids' rooms and a playroom. They were the spookiest of all, the most forsaken-looking, with their pink and blue furniture gone to seed, toys left hurriedly to become discolored with age and neglect.

At the far end of the hall there were two doors. I opened one and the room inside was a different story. This one was being used. It wasn't anything you expect to see in a home-furnishing magazine, but at least it was clean, to some degree cared for. I spotted a photograph of the big blonde on a chest of drawers. This was it, this was Charlie's room. I went to work to find a clue.

I was there an hour and I found nothing. His clothes were there, plenty of them. Charlie was a natty dresser. He even had his underwear monogrammed. He wore Adler Elevator shoes, but it would have taken more than that to make Charlie as Tall as She Is.

I went through his desk twice, carefully both times, but there was nothing there that made any sense either. It was the usual stuff you find in desk drawers: old bank statements, yellowed stationery, and unexplained and uninteresting bits of paper with pencil notations. There was a photograph in the bottom of the drawer of a woman and two little kids. That made sense. That would have to be Ruth Moy and the children whose rooms I had seen down the hall. But there was nothing else.

Suddenly, voices were close to me. I hadn't been on my toes. It didn't occur to me to listen for sounds of people in the empty house. When I heard the voices in the hall there was only time to do one thing, duck in the closet and get lost in the collection of padded suits. My heart was beating so loud that for a minute I couldn't distinguish the voices or hear the words they were saying.

Then I recognized the soft, swishing sound of the ballet dancer. The other voice was Charlie's.

"You're crazy to take a chance," the ballet dancer was saying. "You know what he would say if you asked him."

Charlie grunted something.

"It's just nuts to give her a chance to talk. She may know a lot more than we think. It would be easy to get rid of her. What if she talks, what if she has time to tell what she knows? What do you think he would do to you then?"

"You, you always want to kill someone. I don't think it's smart. Not yet."

"You know what they'll do to you if anything goes wrong now, don't you? Back to China. They'll send you on a trip to see your mother. Only you'll never come back, Charlie. You'll never see your mother and you'll never come back. He'll do it, you know he will. We can't take a chance now, not when we're about to get the big stuff through. It's only another day and then we'll be done. Polyton said definitely that the big breakthrough is coming tomorrow. Then we get our dough. You can't let a little dame spoil it for us."

I was remembering what Jenkins had been saying about Chloe only a couple of hours ago. "If they think she's been planted there to watch anyone, I wouldn't give you a plugged nickel for her life." This was it, this was the beginning of the plan to get rid of her. I was powerless. It would have been so easy to open the closet door and let both of them have it. Two bullets would have made the world a lot healthier place to live in. But not healthy enough; that was the point. The big man, the big brains—he was my assignment, and until I had him, until I knew who he was, I couldn't risk eliminating anyone who might lead me to him, nor could I reveal my identity to anyone.

"You're not smart, Pete," Charlie was saying. "You're not smart at all. Maybe you know a lot. Books and stuff. But you're not smart. What if we try to knock her off and something goes wrong? It's liable to louse up the whole thing. And for what? For nothing, maybe. Maybe she's just a dumb broad who don't know nothing."

"You're going to be sorry, Charlie. It's going to make a whole lot of difference. I could force you to let me kill her if I wanted to. There's a way of making you do things you don't want to."

There was silence for a minute.

"Stop dancing around, you fruit. What are you talking about? What do you mean?"

"If something does go wrong and you decide to take off, hide out somewhere, and he wanted to get you, I know a way of making you come back. I could tell him about your wife and kids. I could tell him where they are. If he got hold of them …"

Pete stopped talking. There was a shuffling and the minute it lasted I shifted position so I could look through the keyhole. Charlie had made a lunge at Pete, but Pete could take care of himself, all right. With one hand he held Charlie in the air. Charlie's feet were dangling as though he were strung up on a noose.

"I was going to save that for later, Charlie. I was going to save that for when I wanted more money than you're planning on giving me. You wouldn't want anything to happen to your family, would you, Charlie?"

"Let go of me, you bastard."

"Oh, Charlie, you don't want to get nasty to me, do you? Not with what I know." He let go of Moy and Moy fell to the floor. "I was going to save that until later, Charlie. But if you don't get rid of the girl, maybe there won't be any later. Maybe the payoff won't come. I don't want to take that chance."

"You like nothing but kill, kill, kill. I tell you, it's not smart. Not yet, anyway."

"Okay, Charlie. Don't say I didn't warn you."

The telephone rang. Charlie moved slowly to answer it. He picked it up, said, "Hello," and then just listened. When he hung up he looked over at Pete, who had spread himself out on the bed. "That was it," Charlie said. "Go ahead. Get rid of the girl."

Pete jumped up. "Was that him?"

Charlie nodded.

"He said to get rid of her?"

"Yes. He says fast. I got instructions."

"I told you so." He began dancing around the room, saying "I told you so" over and over again in a sing-song voice. The phone call meant one thing to me: whether she was aware of it or not, Chloe knew the head man. Or at least she knew enough to be damn close to knowing who he was. They were smart, these boys, and Charlie was right. They wouldn't take a chance knocking her off unless she was really a threat. I had to get to her before they got to her. For a couple of reasons. Business first; I had my job to do. It was a big job and I was going to knock it off right.

"How do I do it, Charlie? What did he say?"

"She's at a print shop now, reading proofs. It's at Eight-twenty-eight Fargo Street. Third floor. She'll be alone up there. The presses make a lot of noise. Do it however you want. Only don't get caught."

"Don't get caught! Do I ever?"

"Use your head this time. Don't get scared away by a door-bell. Don't leave evidence. You almost got in a mess last night because you wanted to get worked up before you killed that girl. Don't take any chances that aren't absolutely necessary. You got that through your head?"

"Maybe I'll use a razor blade," Pete said. "I've never done it with a razor blade. I bet I could do it with one stroke across her throat." He made a gesture of cutting a throat. He was a great one, that boy. A real, clean-cut cutie.

"You better get moving. He said to work fast." I saw Pete getting ready to go. I didn't know what to do. I had to clear out, get to Chloe before Pete did. But I had to do it without exposing myself. That was the trick. If they both left, I had a chance. If Charlie stayed, it was going to take some doing, to knock him out without being seen.

Pete left but Charlie stayed, and I was spending valuable seconds watching him, waiting for him to maneuver himself into a position so I could jump out of the closet and knock him out before he had a chance to see me.

It was torture for me. I knew how important each minute was. Moy was nervous and wouldn't sit still. Every time he got his back to me and was close enough for me to jump, he moved again. All the while I was hearing the sound of my heart and the sound of my watch ticking off the time, letting the dancer get nearer to Chloe.

When the moment came it came fast, and I flew out and clonked him with the butt of my gun in one movement. I don't think he saw me. He turned his head but it was too late. He fell to the floor, blood oozing from the wound. For a minute I was scared that I had killed him, that in my anxiety I had hit him too hard. I leaned down over his chest but he was still breathing. I looked at the bump on his head. It was only a superficial cut, nothing serious. He'd have a hell of a headache when he woke up, but that's about all.

I went through his pockets quickly. He carried a wad of dough and a driver's license. Otherwise he was clean as a whistle. There was something familiar-looking about the tie he was wearing. I looked at the label. It said, "Pure Silk, Made in France." I had to smile. That Jacques sure got around, and I was thinking that he was quite a salesman. He must have hijacked that Chinaman for plenty. I could hardly wait until I saw him. I was going to give him the business about that, make him split the profit.

But that was for later. First, I had to stop the ballet dancer. I had to get Chloe out of danger. I didn't know the name of the print shop, I only knew the address. There wasn't time to try to find out the name and call there to warn her. I had to move faster than that. I dialed the fire department.

When they answered I sounded breathless. "Eight-twenty-eight Fargo," I panted. "Terrible fire. Hurry. Send lots of engines. It's going big. Hurry! Hurry! Eight-twenty-eight Fargo." I hung up. Charlie began to move. I got my shoes out of the closet, put on the right one, and placed it strategically on Charlie's stomach. He stopped moving for a while.

After that I ran fast, out of the house the same way I had come in. I found a cab, flashed a twenty-dollar bill in the driver's face, gave him the Fargo Street address, and told him to stop for nothing. *Nothing.*

CHAPTER EIGHT

The Fire Department had the street blocked off. I got out of the cab at the corner and ran down the block. There was great confusion in front of the Chief Printing Company. The city had sent its best equipment for this fire. It stood in readiness looking wonderfully red and shiny in the afternoon sunlight. People were emptying out of all the exits from the building. A big crowd had circled the place. Firemen, in small groups, were searching frantically for the fire, running in every direction, adding to the bedlam.

I kept watching for Chloe to be in the stream of workers coming out of the doors. I stood deep in the crowd, using it as a cover. I didn't want to chance being seen by the ballet dancer if he were around. By my watch I waited five minutes and still there was no sign of Chloe. The building seemed to be empty except for the firemen.

The sun was hitting the third-floor windows so that there wasn't a chance of seeing into them from any position. Chloe would have been up there. Finally I said to hell with caution; this girl's life was at stake. I made a beeline for the fire escape, planning to climb up to the third floor. A cop caught me just as I was about to go up.

"Wait a minute, buddy, there's a fire in there. You can't go up."

"There's somebody in danger there." I tried to pull myself free. "I've got to go up."

"If anyone is in danger up there, the fire department will take care of them. Now, get back in line."

I made a break from him again but suddenly there were two cops, one on each arm, and they were strong enough to hold me motionless. I looked up for a moment, long enough to see Chloe run out on the fire escape and then be pulled back in quickly. They were up there and there was still time.

"Up there," I screamed. "Third floor. The fire is up there. Third floor. Turn your hoses up there." I yelled the same thing over and over again, at the top of my lungs, until I heard the sound of the hoses hit the windows and felt the sprays of water reflected from the side of the building.

They had turned the hoses on full blast and the firemen started streaming up. Hell really broke loose then. People were scurrying around like ants at a picnic.

In the middle of the tumult, I saw the ballet dancer walk out of the building, carrying Chloe in his arms. I didn't know if she were dead or just knocked out. He walked slowly, almost casually, headed toward the street corner. I kept pace with him fifty feet away, elbowing my way through the crowd. I couldn't figure out his plan, I didn't know what he was heading for. If Chloe were dead he would have dumped the body or left it upstairs in the printing shop. If she weren't dead, then he was kidnaping her. And a very sweet job he was doing of it. Everyone who saw him carrying her thought he was a big hero. He had rescued a girl and was taking her to safety. Only I knew the real story, and I was powerless to stop him. I couldn't reveal myself to him in this crowd. I decided that if I had to show myself to save Chloe, I would have to make sure he'd never have a chance to expose me to anyone else.

"Is there a doctor here? Somebody get a doctor! Quick, a doctor! That girl! That girl needs a doctor. Quick! Quick!" I kept well into the crowd as I shouted. My knees were bent so that I wouldn't stand out in the mass of people. The screaming did the trick. The crowd's attention was focused on Chloe, and there was a general shifting movement toward her. The people circled the ballet dancer, blocking his escape. He was trapped. A man stepped forward. "I'm a doctor," he said.

The ballet dancer lowered Chloe to the ground. As the doctor began to examine her, Pete backed away from the crowd, moving almost imperceptibly toward the end of it, and then he took off fast. I watched him all the way and made sure he was gone before I dared edge close enough to find out what had happened to the girl.

She wasn't dead. Pete had evidently knocked her out. "She must have hit her head on something," the doctor was saying. "No damage that I can see. You got to X-ray, though. You've always got to X-ray in cases like this. Stand back. Give the lady air."

I let the crowd back up behind me. Some foresighted person had a pint of bourbon in his back pocket. He offered it to the doctor. The doctor poured it down Chloe's throat. She came to after a little while. "You're all right, young lady?"

Chloe shook her head. Her eyes opened—and they were big and they were full of fright. "What happened?"

"You tell us," the doctor said. "This man here" (he pointed toward the place where Pete had been standing but he didn't lift his eyes to notice that Pete was gone) "carried you out of the building. What happened?"

Chloe searched fearfully for Pete. In searching for him, she spotted me. She started to call to me but I put my finger to my lips. She looked past me then.

"I must have fainted," she said. "The fire engines. I heard the engines and I was way up on the third floor. I'm awfully frightened of fire engines. When I was a kid once I was in a fire and it was terrible." She was sitting up, looking more alive. The crowd had expected blood. When they saw she was all right they began drifting away. Then a fight started between a cop and a fireman over near the building and the whole crowd shifted at once to that spot. I moved with them, staying at the back, as close as I could to where Chloe was.

The doctor said something to her and she shook her head. He helped her stand up. The first minute she was wobbly but after a few minutes she seemed to get control of herself and was steadier. She walked toward the commotion, becoming caught in the crowd watching the fight. When she was next to me, I whispered, "Wait five minutes. Walk to the next corner, southwest side of the street, and get into a cab. I'll be in it."

She moved forward in the crowd. I counted silently to ten, then took off. When I got to the corner, there was a cab there, but unfortunately no driver. He must have been over at the false alarm. I got in and lay on the floor.

A few minutes later the door of the cab opened and Chloe got in. She was startled at first. "Get in and sit down," I said.

She giggled, wrinkling up her nose the way I like it. "You look so silly, Maguire. You're so big and the floor is so small."

"You all right?"

"Yes, I guess so." She rubbed her head. "He hit me."

"I figured that. You're lucky you're living. He was out for murder."

When I said the word "murder," her whole expression changed. Fear came back into her eyes, her lips trembled.

"Johnny," she said. Her voice was low, tight. "Hold my hand, hold it hard."

"What's the matter?" I looked up at her. She was about to pass out. She grabbed my hand. The pressure of it was tremendous for such a little girl. Her nails were digging into me. It came suddenly, a scream that filled the tiny taxi and hung in the air like an echo in a cave. She had begun to cry softly before the sound of the scream had faded away.

"Take it easy, baby. You're all right now. You're all right." I let her cry it out.

"It was awful, Johnny." She shook her head, not believing what was still so vivid in her mind. "I can't tell you how awful it was. I mean, I'm not afraid—I suppose you have to expect to die—but not the way he tried. That look. The way his eyes looked. You've never seen anyone look that way." She shook her head again. "He had so much time. If he had wanted to kill me he could have used a gun. It would have been over quickly. But he was playing with me, Johnny. He had a razor and he was playing, enjoying it. It was awful, awful. He had the queerest expression— so depraved-looking. I can't describe it exactly. It was..."

"Never mind, little one. Don't even try. I know."

She cried harder and was shivering. I pulled her roughly to the floor of the cab, on top of me, and held her tight against me, trying to let the heat of my body warm her, the strength of my arms stop the shivering. "I'll never forget it," she whispered. "I'll never forget that look on his face. I'll see it always. I'll live in fear of it."

"No, you won't. He's going to be dead. I'll personally see to that. He's going to be dead. I'll show him to you when he's dead."

"Johnny, I'm scared."

"Would you like to get out of all this?"

She didn't say anything. The trembling began to fade in intensity. She pulled away from me, sat up on the seat, ran a comb through her hair, and put on some lipstick. Asking her if she wanted to get out of this was posing a challenge. She took the challenge and it gave her strength, pulled her together.

"What about it?" I repeated. "Would you like to get out of this?"

She shook her head. "No. Not now, anyway. Maybe when it's over, when I've done the job I'm supposed to be doing, then I'll get out. Not now."

I shifted around on the floor. There was a hump in the middle that was killing my back. "It may be too late. Have you thought of that? You know too much, Chloe. I don't know what it is that you know, and you don't either, but they aren't going to stop until they find out. Maybe you ought to get out now, while there's still time."

"I don't want to, Maguire. It wouldn't do me any good if I did. They'd find me no matter where I went. Let me finish whatever this is that I'm mixed up in. Let me finish it and let it be over. I don't want to live in fear for the rest of my life."

"Okay. Just so long as you know what the score is," I said.

She smiled at me as though I were a little boy. "I've known what the score is for a long time, Maguire."

It could have meant a lot of things. She could have been talking about us. There was something there between us, unsaid, not known in words. It was a current running between us, a current of excitement, of expectation. I was feeling it and I was convinced that she was feeling it too. It was made sharper and more alive by the danger we were in. I thought about love again. I was looking up at the ripped, dirty ceiling of the taxicab and was thinking about love.

Chloe said, "The cab driver is coming. Where shall I tell him to go?"

I thought for a minute. I had to hide her somewhere, make sure that she would be safe. "Tell him to go to the Payton Hotel, Forty-third and Latoon. Keep watching out the back window to see if the cab is being followed. If it is, signal me." The cab driver opened the door.

"Been waiting long, miss?"

"I want to go to the Payton Hotel, Forty-third and Latoon."

He started the engine. "The what?"

"The Payton Hotel, Forty-third and—"

"I know where it is, miss. I just wanted to make sure you wanted to go there." He ground his gears and started moving.

I didn't blame the driver for wondering about Chloe's wanting to go to the Payton Hotel. It was quite a dive. I knew about it because I got mixed up with a girl one night when I was too far gone to know what I was doing. I woke up the next morning, rolled, in a dingy room at this hotel. I remembered thinking at the time it would be a good place for a hideout. One thing I knew, there wasn't even going to be a raised eyebrow when Chloe and I walked in without luggage and asked for a room.

She kept checking out the back window to see if we were being followed. Evidently the coast was clear, but I stayed on the floor until we were a safe distance away. I got up quietly and sat down next to her. My back felt like hell. I had been in the same position for almost half an hour. Chloe wanted to hold hands, so we held hands. The driver looked back at her through the rear-view mirror. When he saw me sitting next to her his teeth nearly fell out. "Where did you come from, bud?"

I smiled. "I've been here."

"You could have fooled me, miss," he said. "Where did you hide him, in your pocket?" He reached over and clicked the meter to register an additional passenger.

Neither Chloe nor I said anything. Every time I looked over at her she was smiling at me. It was infectious. Pretty soon I was smiling too. Like a high-school boy.

As I expected, the desk clerk didn't raise an eyebrow when we walked in and asked for a double room. What surprised me was that Chloe didn't either. She didn't make the usual maidenly protests.

The room wasn't as bad as I thought it would be. It was big and the sun was coming in brightly through the double window. I slipped the clerk, who had shown us up to the room, a half buck and locked the door after him.

Chloe sat on the bed, kicked off her shoes, and stretched her arms. She looked at me brightly. "Hello, Maguire."

"Hello," I said. Then I hesitated. "Are you all right?"

"Yes, I'm just fine." She lowered her eyes for a minute. "Are you all right?"

"Sure, I'm all right." Then neither of us said anything. I knew that what was going to happen was inevitable. It was first in importance. We both wanted it, Chloe in her way and I in mine. As tired as I was, I ached to have her. It was more than the brightness of her face, the novelty of the sweet young thing sitting on the bed. I needed to be having her as an alcoholic needs to have a drink. There were these things and they were functioning inside me at once. I knew it was going to happen, I knew that we were both wanting it to happen, and until it happened there would be no room to do this other thing, to find out what she knew that would lead me to the head of the spy ring and to Tom White's killer.

I had come to the hotel to hide her out, to have a chance to probe her about the operation at *United World.* But this other thing was there, as prominent as a third person would have been in the room. Until we had worked it out, there was no time for questioning.

"What are you thinking about, Maguire?" She lay back on the bed, staring at the ceiling.

"Nothing. Nothing much. I was wondering what you must be thinking."

"About what? About you?"

"In a way. Yes. About me."

"I think you're fine."

"I don't mean that. I mean about bringing you here. To this place."

"Why did you?"

"To hide you out. I want to keep you from getting knocked off by that ballet dancer. They won't stop until they get you. They think you know too much. They don't think they're safe until you're out of the way. They have to get rid of you." I was aware that I was talking too fast, saying words that I had said before. The sounds of my words were low and thick, the way a voice gets when your insides are contracting with wanting. I stopped talking, lighted a cigarette, and walked to the window. The street was dotted with the disillusioned people walking in disillusioned rhythm. "Why are you being the way you are?"

"How am I being?"

I wasn't looking at her but I was knowing how she was. The picture of her on the bed was vivid in my mind. "You want me as much as I want you," I said. "The whole part of it. The sex part too."

Her voice was almost a whisper. "Yes," she said. "Why do you think it's so strange?"

"You're not the type. You're not the kind to take sex casually, just for the hell of it, just because you want it. You're the kind who wants it with trimmings. Marriage and security."

"Why don't you look at me when you talk, Maguire?"

"Look, little one, I'm not the kind of guy you're used to. I'm not bred to play games and make conversation for what I want. When I see what I want, I grab it and take it."

"And that's why you won't look at me? Because you'll see what you want and grab it and take it?"

I didn't say anything. There was a scamp of a kid pulling a beat-up red wagon down the street, the wagon filled with newspapers. It was getting to be that time of day, when evening papers are delivered.

"You wanted to know, Maguire, why I'm being like I am, not ashamed that I want you as much as you want me. There's a good reason for it. I waited before when I loved someone. I waited through a war, and then there wasn't anything to wait for. I wanted him. Physically. I'm not afraid to say it. But I waited because I was all mixed up with standards and social procedures. I never knew what it was to go to bed with the man I loved. I don't want that to happen now. I've just brushed death. Close enough to feel the breath of it. And it's not over. Not yet. Not for either of us. We both have jobs to finish. If I come through, maybe you won't. Our business is danger. I don't want to risk losing my chance again. I want all of love this time."

"What's this talk about love? How come you love me? You've known me since this morning. How can you know whether you love me?"

"I suppose I don't know, really. I mean maybe I just think I love you. It may be a lot of things. But right now, right this minute, I believe I love you. That's enough for me."

"What do you want me to say? Do you want me to say that I love you?"

"No. You don't have to say it. You never say it, do you, Maguire? A man like you never says that he's in love. It doesn't matter. It doesn't change the way I feel."

I lowered one window shade. "It's wrong to talk like this now, you know that. I have a job to do and you have a job to do. It's not just any job. It's important. It may mean human lives."

"Right now, it's not as important as you and me. Nothing is. It sounds terrible to say it, but it's the way I feel. In the last few years, my life has been all of that, all working for peace and working to save human lives from futile destruction. Now I want time for myself, for what I want. For what I want inside."

I lowered the other window shade and the room was almost in darkness. I dropped the cigarette to the floor and mashed it into the worn, threadbare carpet. Then I turned to face her.

She was standing up, waiting for me. We met halfway across the room, holding each other tightly, shaking with our still leashed wantings, gasping the stale hotel air between kisses. I guess, at that moment, I wanted her as much as I ever wanted anything.

This was what I wanted, this was the love and the wanting occurring at the same moment, each one pointing up and making more poignant the other. And yet as I held her, aware that every part of me was ready for her, I knew that it should not happen. I wasn't her kind of guy. I was going to louse up her whole life for this one quick burst of passion. It didn't make sense. "I can't," I said. "I can't do this."

"What is it, Johnny? What's the matter?"

I tried to break away. She held fast to me. It took force. My back was to her. She touched me and I moved away again. "Don't, Chloe. Don't touch me. Please."

"What happened, Johnny?"

"This is a damn hard thing for me to do," I began. "I'm going to be heroic." Then I almost whispered the words: "I'm going to be decent."

"You don't want me," she said. I heard the squeak of the bed as she sat down. "You don't want me, that's it."

"I want you very much. You'll never know how much I want you. But I'm not for you and you're not for me. You've never known anyone like me before. I'm all physical.... I don't even know how to talk to you, Chloe. I'm not in your league. I don't know the polite words to say what I want to say."

"Then don't use polite words."

"This wouldn't mean anything to me, going to bed with you. It wouldn't mean anything but another roll in the hay for me, just another hash mark to put in my little black book—seen and conquered."

"I don't believe you, Johnny. I think it means more than that. I wouldn't be feeling the way I do if there weren't something inside you. Something besides sex."

I was trying to think of nothing, to become lost in nothingness, to let the words I thought I ought to be saying come out as a rehearsed speech. "You're wrong, Chloe. This has got nothing to do with love or feelings. It's not that I haven't any feelings for you—I think you're a nice kid. But as far as I'm concerned, this is straight sex, pure and simple." There was the feel of her hand on my back, soft and exploratory. Every nerve ending in my body was alerted, waiting. I held still for her. First there was one hand, then both hands, then her face against my back.

"You're sweet, Maguire. You're a sweet guy and you're a terrible liar."

"Okay, so I'm a liar."

"What are you trying to do, tell me that I should save myself for the man I love?"

"I don't want to spoil anything for you. There's going to be a guy for you some day, the kind you grew up with. You'll be in love with him and he'll be in love with you. I don't want to spoil that moment for you—or for him."

"What if I said that I loved you, that you were the one I've been waiting for?"

"It wouldn't be true. You might think it's true. Maybe right now I think it's true. For this one moment maybe we do love each other. But it won't last."

"I don't care, Johnny. Let me take it now, while there's still time. Don't let me lose my chance again. Do that for me."

"The most important thing I can do for you is to make sure that there will be more time, a lifetime for you. I can do that by doing my job, by breaking up the spy ring. When this danger is over and we aren't thrown together by fright and the shadow of death, you'll see me as I am and I'll see you as a punk kid from Iowa. We'd be embarrassed and sorry."

"I'd never be sorry," she whispered. "Never, never be sorry."

"Let me do this my way. Let me do something decent, will you? Let me use my head instead of my—heart."

Slowly, grudgingly she took her hands away from me and finally her face. "All right, Maguire. If that's the way it has to be."

I raised the window shades. The late-afternoon sun came into the room at an oblique angle, bisecting the room into lightness and darkness. "First of all," I said, "I think maybe you ought to know what this whole thing is about, how *United World* fits into the picture of spies and. atomic information getting out of the country."

"Johnny?"

"What?"

"Can you just turn it on and off like that, turn from love to business as quickly as you would flick on a light?"

Wanting that had not come to fruition hung heavy inside my body. I was thinking I was getting soft in the head, passing this up. I had only to reach out and take it. I ignored her question, went on talking about the spy setup, brought it up to date for her. "Your friend Polyton contacts the head of this organization directly or he deals with a very close go-between. Think now, think carefully. Who does Polyton see?"

"He sees so many people. People on the magazine mostly. It's so hard to believe that he can be a traitor. He's such a nice old man."

"The hell with his being a nice old man. Forget about how you feel about anything. Facts. Concentrate on facts. I'm not going to break this thing without facts. Who does Polyton see? Name their names."

"I don't see what—"

"I'm not asking you to see anything. You're working for me now. Say what I tell you to say and nothing more. Who does Polyton see?"

She started naming names, talking softly, hurt by the anger that had been in my voice. The names didn't mean much even after she explained who they were. I remembered everything carefully, even what seemed unimportant on the surface.

"Are there any Chinese people who come to see Polyton?"

"No, I don't think so. There are so many people in the office all the time. From all over the world. But I can't think of anyone who appears regularly enough to be the man you mean."

"What about going out? Does Polyton leave the office much?"

"Not even for lunch. He brings his lunch. That's the most remarkable thing about him. He's really just a volunteer worker. I mean he has a retirement pension and isn't obligated to work at all. But he's more regular than any of the other employees. He's always on time and works late, overtime very often."

Early darkness was beginning, a reminder that summer was over and the winter coming. I still didn't have the answer. "Tell me again who comes to see him. Name them all again."

"Oh, Johnny, I'm so tired. I've been through so much. Let me lie down a minute and rest."

"Stay on your feet. Stay where you are and do as I say. Name them again. Go through the names again."

"You're a hateful man, John Maguire."

"Am I?"

"I know you're doing a job. But you're making it miserable for me and you don't have to. You're angry because what you call your sense of decency won't let you have me. It's made everything turn sour." She came toward me and threw her arms around me. "Can't you see, Johnny, that I want it? I want you. It isn't shameful. I'm a good girl, Johnny. I'm decent. But I want you to make love to me. I want to know what love is before I die."

"You're not going to die." I held back every impulse, every beating of my blood, wanting me to hold her tightly. "You're not going to die. I promise you that. They got one person who was close to me but they won't get you. Not this time. I'm on my toes this time. Now, get back to the other side of the room."

"Kiss me first."

"What's the use, what's the point?" But her lips were too fast for me and the magnetism of them too strong. When the kiss was over she drew away shyly, went back to the other side of the room, and went through the names she knew of the people Polyton saw. She had forgotten some in the second recital and remembered some others.

I was amused by her description of Jacques Marples. "There was a Frenchman," she said, "sort of the Charles Boyer type with more hair. He was awfully attractive. That's why I remember him." It was much the same thing Tina had said about Jacques. He got around, that guy. I thought it would be a good idea to compare notes with him, too. I wasn't getting anywhere with Chloe; the answer hadn't come out yet. I was covering ground that Jacques already seemed to have covered. I decided to try to find him. There was a bar where he went sometimes. I had never been there but I knew where it was.

"You can forget about the Frenchman," I said as I moved toward the door. "His name is Jacques Marples, and he's a very good friend of mine. In fact, he's working on our side."

"Where are you going, Maguire?"

"Out," I said. "I've got to see a man."

"I'm sorry," she said.

"About what?"

"About everything. About not being able to help you."

"Look, Chloe, while I'm gone, make a list. List everyone over again. Make notes about each person you know anything about."

"All right, Johnny."

"For no reason leave this room. If anyone knocks at the door, don't answer it. If the phone rings, don't answer it. I'll be back as soon as I can."

"All right."

"I'll bring you some food. You'll be hungry by then."

"Yes, I guess I will. Johnny?"

"Huh?"

"Don't let anything happen to you. Be careful. Remember what you promised. You can't do it if you're dead."

"The Irish don't die so easy."

"About the other thing, about us—when this is over and everything is all right maybe we ought to talk about it again. I mean about you and me."

"Maybe," I said. "Maybe."

CHAPTER NINE

I wasted twenty-five minutes of valuable time in the Surfside Bar waiting for Jacques. The bartender knew him, all right, but said he didn't usually come in until after midnight. I called Tina at her office, not realizing it was after working hours. I rang her up at home then.

"Tina?"

"Well, Counselor, where've you been?"

"Working," I said. "Do you know if there were any phone messages for me this afternoon?"

"No, I don't think so. You sound frantic. Anything the matter?"

"Nothing is the matter. I just couldn't get to a phone before now."

"I'm sure there weren't. Phyllis would have told me. She suspects that I see you outside of the office."

"A very clever girl, this Phyllis."

"You aren't planning on coming up, are you? I look a sight. My chin is in a sling. I had a good look at myself today in a strong light. I think I'm beginning to sag. I don't look my best, greased and tied up."

"I won't be able to get over tonight. I'll see you sometime tomorrow," I said. "Keep your chin up."

"Very funny, Counselor. Very funny and not at all."

There was a chance that Jacques had left some word for me at my apartment. I was close enough to scoot over there and check.

Right after I closed the door to the apartment, as I was reaching for the light switch, I realized that someone was in the apartment. I drew my gun and fell to the floor. I waited for some sound. After a minute there was a gentle clinking of a glass. I stood up and flicked on the light. Jacques was sitting on the couch, smiling and drinking my brandy.

"Why didn't you say something? You scared the hell out of me."

He laughed. Maybe he was the Boyer type. I figured I'd keep him away from Tina. I'd trust him with my dough and my life, but not with my girl. "It is good practice, Johnny. You did very well. I could not have shot you quickly enough. You fell to the floor too soon."

"You going to put a gold star on my report card, teacher? Let me have some of that brandy."

He poured and I drank one quickly, then sipped the second glass.

"How does it go, Johnny?"

"I don't know. I got the job I wanted, if that means anything. I've got a clear field to go ahead and break up the spy ring, bring in the head man."

"I am glad for you, Johnny. It was what I thought when Biget sent for you."

"I'm not sure that I'm getting anywhere. Every alley I go up seems to be a blind one. You've been working on this case too, Jacques. I think the time has come to pool our information. What do you know about this guy Polyton?"

"Polyton?"

"Sure, the old gent who works for *United World*. You know him. Chloe says she's seen you up there talking to him. Have you any idea who his contacts are? I don't mean the people who give him the information, I mean the people who get it from him."

"I do not know, Johnny. I did not know until now that this man is part of it. I was making the routine investigation. I know nothing about this."

I explained the setup briefly to Jacques. "That's the way it works. I hoped that maybe you would have the answer. Both Charlie Moy and Polyton contact the key man. Can you think of anything that might help me, any lead I can follow?"

"This Chloe, she knows nothing?"

"Sure she does. She must know. It's only a question of time before she figures it out. I've got her locked up in a room at the Payton Hotel trying to put two and two together. They tried to knock her off earlier this afternoon. I'm hiding her out at this hotel. Are you sure that you can't give me any tips on this thing?"

"I would like to help, Johnny. I would like to have an idea, but..." He shrugged his shoulders.

"Okay, Jacques. I guess I'd better try something else. I'll go back and see if Chloe has the thing figured out yet."

"First, I have another message for you from Biget."

"From Biget?"

"You are surprised?"

"Yes. I thought I was on my own. I didn't expect to hear from him until I finished the job."

"It is a lead, maybe. I do not know. You are to go to Fifty-six Hawthorne Street."

"That's Moy's address."

"I did not know. Biget said for you to go there."

"And do what?"

"That I thought you would know. The instructions read, 'Message center, third floor.' To me it means nothing."

"It means plenty to me," I said. "That must be where the stuff is passed out of the country. Something like that. What a jerk I am! I should have searched that house today, instead of wasting so much time in Charlie's room. Only I wonder why Biget wants me to go there. What's the point of it? We can always clean that up later, after we catch the head of the organization."

"In this business, Johnny, there is much we do not understand until it is over."

"I guess you're right. When am I supposed to go?"

"At once. As soon as I made contact with you."

"Maybe they think I'll find the lead there. Could be. I'll try it, anyway. The coast ought to be clear. Moy will be at the Chinese Keyhole by now."

"Everything is in such a hurry these days," Jacques said. "Stay a minute and we can drink together."

"I'd like to, Jacques, but I've got to keep moving."

"It's been a long time, Johnny, since we have been drunk together. We do not sing unless we are drunk. In France we sing all the time, drunk or sober."

"Go on, Frenchie. In France you never spend a sober minute."

"Maybe, when you have taken this man, this head of the organization, we will have time again for the fun we used to have."

"Sure we will. If I break up this spy ring, I'll get a bigger job. Bigger job means bigger pay. Bigger pay means more brandy." I laughed. "It's funny, Jacques. I'm so close to knowing who this guy is. The clues to him are everywhere I go. I know that, and yet I just can't get hold of the right thing."

"It is possible that it is so simple you cannot see it, Johnny. Maybe you are too close to it to see it. It happens that way sometimes."

"Maybe you're right. I'll get it, all right. I've got to. And now I'd better get moving."

I went into my bedroom and put on a clean shirt. The slug they took out of Tom White's back lay on the dresser. I looked at it for a moment and then slipped it into my pocket. It won't be long, Tom, I was thinking. It's getting close, boy. It's getting close.

Jacques was still coddling the brandy, swishing it around in his glass, sipping it slowly. "What are you going to do, Jacques?"

"I do not know. I will see you later. Somewhere. Maybe I'll wait here."

"Wish me luck."

"Good luck, Johnny. Good luck."

CHAPTER TEN

The night had become complete in its darkness. It hadn't begun to rain yet, but a storm was threatening silently. I wasn't particularly keyed up about going back to Moy's house.

I didn't much see the point of Biget insisting I go back to the house to rip up the spy's message center. Granted, breaking up the message center was important, but I couldn't figure out why it had priority over tracking down the big brains. I was so hot on the trail, I begrudged every minute that I had to spend on a tangent, and I thought this assignment was a tangent. On the other hand, Biget knew what he was doing. Maybe, I thought, the answer would be there.

There was no light anywhere in the house. I checked carefully from all sides before I slid through the basement window and went upstairs in the darkness. In spite of the fact that I knew what to expect, the deserted Chinese horror house still gave me the creeps. Burning match after match, I stumbled up the stairs.

On the second floor, I looked in Charlie's room to see if he had picked himself up from the floor. I flicked on the lights for a moment. He was gone, all right, but there was a dried spot of blood on the carpeting. Charlie had never known who hit him.

I found the stairway to the attic without any trouble. I groped for the light switch, found it, and flicked it, but nothing happened. I cursed myself for not bringing a flashlight, lighted another match, and started up the stairs. Near the top, the match burned down. I started to strike another when I heard a sound. I froze and waited. The sound might have been anything, the momentary flapping of a shutter, a mouse, simply the creaking sound that old houses sometimes make. But I had to be cautious.

When, after a few minutes, the sound was not repeated, I started up the remaining stairs, but on hands and knees this time, making as little sound as possible. The top board of the staircase was loose and squeaked loudly when I hit it. Almost simultaneously with the creak of the board there was the sharp whang of a bullet sailing over my head. Lucky that I hadn't been standing up.

I flopped on my belly, lay flat, and drew my gun.

"You are too careful." The voice came from the other end of the room. It was Moy's voice. I figured he must have heard me come into the house, guessed where I was heading, and had been up there waiting for me. "You should have lit another match. If you had lit one more match, you would be dead now. You are too careful."

I didn't say a word. I knew that he was waiting to hear the sound of my voice so that he could locate my position. I edged forward a little and then to the left.

The odds were against me but I had a chance. In order to shoot me, Charlie would have to find me. If he turned on a light to find me, the chances were that I could plug him first. But he knew the room, he knew where things were in the room. If I ran into something, he could locate me by the sound.

"I did not expect you back so soon," Charlie said. "I was not ready."

That may have meant anything. It may have meant that there was a leak in our plans, that he had the tip-off that I was coming. Or it may have meant that he figured whoever clonked him that afternoon would be back to find out what else the house was being used for. Whatever had happened wasn't important at this point. I had to get out.

I waited for him to talk again. My ears were getting adjusted and I figured if he spoke some more I could locate his position.

But when he spoke again his voice came from the other end of the room. He had moved noiselessly. By using my elbows I shoved myself forward. I ran into something and there was a crackling noise. I rolled over fast and in the split second there was the flare of fire and the sound of the gun.

I didn't shoot back. He was smart. He had moved too. I felt in front of me. I had hit against a big object on the floor. When I felt the locks, I knew it was a trunk of some kind. I took cover behind it.

"It's too bad there's not more time," he said. "We have a crack on the head to settle up. In China there would be time to settle this like gentlemen. I could be even with you, crack on the head for crack on the head. But in your country, there's no time for this. Everything is always too much of a rush." He had been moving as he talked. I kept my eye sharp for a patch of white somewhere. His head would be bandaged where I had hit him. Maybe the patch of white would give him away.

The trunk was metal but I doubted if it would deflect a bullet. But it was better than being out in the open. I pulled a bluff. "Give up, Moy. You haven't got a chance."

He laughed. "You don't know the Chinese. Chinese people have patience. They're not like you Americans. We can wait. You know what you're going to do? You're going to make a break for it soon. You won't be able to stand waiting. I can wait for you to show yourself. I can wait hours and it won't bother me. But it'll start eating you. You're a hothead. You're going to try something, and when you do ..."

In his rough way, Moy was being the Chinese philosopher. He was right. I wasn't constructed to sweat it out and wait for him to make a false move. I had to do something. I was built for action.

"You're a businessman, Moy. I'll make a business deal with you."

For an answer there was another shot of the gun. It was wide. I shot back this time but there was the sound of glass shattering and I knew that I had missed too.

"You were not even close," he said, and laughed again.

"I'll make a deal with you, Moy. Give up, give yourself up, and nothing will happen to your wife and kids." It was a long shot. The ballet dancer had tried it earlier and it had struck home. Maybe it would work again.

"Nothing will happen to them," he said. "You will never have the chance to tell anyone."

"I've had the chance. Ruth Moy, Two-fifty-four Seeley Street. I've had the chance. My headquarters know. If I don't show up in an hour, they have instructions to take them as hostages."

"It is no good. In my country it would maybe scare me. But not here. You wouldn't touch them. They don't do nothing. The law says that you can't hold them. It would be like kidnaping and holding for ransom. It's against your law. The law will let them go. In China we could make a business deal, but not in your country, my friend. In your country the law protects my family."

He had me there. He was too smart for me to pull the bluff successfully. But I needed time, so I kept talking. "What about your kids, don't you care about them? Even if they do get free, everyone will know that their old man is a traitor. How do you think it's going to be for the rest of their lives? All their friends are going to remember that their old man was a traitor."

"No one will remember nothing. They remember who won the World Series this year, but they don't remember that Charlie Moy was a traitor."

"Hey, Charlie."

"What?"

"You're sure I'm going to die, aren't you?"

He laughed. "I'd like to see you get out of this."

"Okay, then tell me something. Tell me how come this house is the way it is."

He didn't answer. I knew that I had hit his sore spot, so I kept after it. "What happened? Why did your wife and kids pull out? It must have been all of a sudden from the looks of the place. What happened?"

"They don't know anything about their old man. The kids don't. They don't remember me no more. She won't let me see them."

"What was it? Did your wife find out you were playing around with another woman? Or did she find out that you were mixed up in shady deals?"

"It don't make no difference why she did what she did. She left, and nothing in the house has been changed since. It's not going to be until she comes back with the kids. It's nobody's business why she run out on me."

"You can tell me, Charlie. I'm going to die. I won't tell anybody."

He had changed his position again. "It was my fault. I make a few bucks and I go for white girls. In China it don't make no difference when you're married. But Ruth she thinks like American women think. So she pulls out. So what? So what do I care?"

"You must care a lot. You've left the house untouched."

"The only thing is about the kids. I don't care about Ruth. Hell, I can get better than her any day of the week. It's only about the kids. She takes good care of the kids. Now, shut up about it."

"They'll get you, Charlie. Even if you get me, they'll get you eventually. We're too close not to get you."

"Tomorrow, it will be too late. Tomorrow I will be on my way to China."

"You're lying. You've got too much dough sunk into the Keyhole to pull out."

"My wife, she will get the money. She will get it for the kids. It is your law."

"What about the blonde? You wouldn't leave her."

"I spit on her. She don't know when she's got it good."

It was the end of my conversational rope. From that point on I knew my life depended on action, not words. We stayed there in the silence and the darkness for a long time. It seemed longer than it actually was. Moy had been right. He could outsit me, all right. I was busting to make a lunge for him, busting for action. But it would have been suicide to try anything at that point.

The phone downstairs started to ring. "You'd better go answer it," I said. "It might be your big boss."

He laughed and there was silence again punctuated by the ringing of the phone.

Slowly, noiselessly, I took off one shoe. I wiggled around on the floor, making sounds as though I were moving. Then I threw the shoe across the floor. He started shooting in the direction of the sound, shot after shot. I jumped up and fired at him across the trunk. I don't know how many shots. I just kept shooting in the direction of the flare of his gun fire.

I heard his gun fall to the floor, then the sound of his body staggering and hitting against a table. I had hit him. It was an old American trick and it had worked. It had outmaneuvered the patience of the Orient. I moved cautiously toward him. My foot kicked against the softness of his body before I saw him.

He was dead. Very dead.

I found an overhead light and turned it on. The attic looked like most people's attics, except that there was a powerful short-wave radio there. The trunk that I had been using as cover was locked. I went through Charlie's pockets and found the keys. At first appearance it seemed to be nothing more than a steamer trunk packed for a trip. But as I pulled it apart, I found small bits of metal, machinery parts, hidden in with the clothes. They were harmless-looking fragments but I knew how important they were and how close they had come to getting out of the country.

There seemed to be something underneath the fabric trunk lining. I ripped it apart. Blueprints, photographs, and drawings fell out. It was six months' work, smuggling these things out of the atomic labs piece by piece. Here they were, all in one place, all ready to go.

I threw everything back into the trunk, locked it again and put the keys in my pocket.

Charlie's gun lay where it had dropped. I picked it up. It was not the same gun that had killed Tom White. It was a different caliber. The man I was after was still at large, still dangerous.

Chloe.

I had forgotten for a minute about Chloe. She was the one who was in danger. I had made a promise to her, a promise that I would be personally responsible for her staying alive. There would always be that pain inside me, a spot of pain for Tom White because he had died instead of me. One thing like that is enough for a man. If something happened to Chloe, that would make two. I couldn't let that happen. I couldn't fail her.

CHAPTER ELEVEN

I was too late. Chloe was gone. The hotel room was in great disorder. She must have put up one hell of a fight. The elevator man and desk clerk had seen nothing; no one came in and no one went out.

Since Moy had been lying in wait for me, I was certain that the ballet dancer had come for Chloe. The question was, where had he taken her? It was a big city; you could spend a lifetime being lost in it. There was no time to be a patient, plodding detective. I had to find out where she was and I had to find out fast.

I knew then that there had been a master plan to all this. I had walked into a trap at Moy's house. And while I was trapped, Chloe had been kidnaped. I knew how Pete worked. He would take her somewhere where he could fool around with her first, take his time about killing her. But where?

The big blonde might know. Charlie Moy knew the plan, but I had killed him. There was a chance that the big blonde would know where Pete had taken Chloe. She was my only chance. I knew I would have to get it out of her in some way, even if I had to beat it out of her.

Every inch of the way across town, I kept my eyes on the road, driving for all I was worth. I parked double in front of the Chinese Keyhole. My friend the doorman said something to me but I didn't hear it. I ran past him and into the club.

Business was as usual at the Keyhole. It was early and not as crowded as it would be later. The headwaiter came up to me. "Is Miss Nevaire in her dressing room?"

"Who wants to know?"

"I want to know, and I want to know fast."

"Who are you?" he asked, and he stood threateningly close to me so that I would be aware of his size and power.

"I'm in a hurry. Is she here or up in her apartment?"

"Wait here," he said.

"Wait nothing." I pushed my way past and went into the main room and headed toward the exit door near the stage, which led back to the dressing rooms. The head-waiter took off after me but he couldn't make too much of a racket because the show was going on.

Backstage there was a long corridor with dressing rooms on either side. I opened a couple of doors quickly before I found the big blonde. She was sitting in front of a mirror putting on fake eyelashes. She was stripped for action but covered loosely with a silk robe. She saw me through the mirror, looked startled for a minute, then ignored me and went on with what she was doing.

The headwaiter burst into the room about five seconds after I did. The blonde said, "It's all right, Gus. He's all right."

"You sure, Gail? He's a wise guy."

"It's all right, Gus. Leave me alone with him." Gus started to leave. "And Gus..."

"Yeah?"

"Tell Violet to stretch out her act tonight. I want some extra time."

"Okay. What about Pete? He ain't showed up yet."

"He'll be here. Don't worry, he'll show up. Has Charlie come in?"

"I ain't seen him."

"As soon as he shows, tell him I want to talk to him."

When Gus had gone she said, "You got a cigarette, bright eyes?"

I tossed her my pack. "Where's Pete?"

She lighted the cigarette slowly, watching the flame of the match before she blew it out. "What do you want with Pete?"

"What's he done with that girl?"

"You know, I didn't believe this."

"You didn't believe what?"

"About you," she said. "I didn't believe that you were a cop or whatever you are."

"Well, now you know it. I want to know what Pete has done with that girl."

"Is she your sweetie?"

"Look, I want that girl before something happens to her."

She stood up, walked to a cabinet, and took out the iron belt that she wore in her act. Except that it wasn't iron, it was some kind of plastic made to look like iron. She slipped it around her waist. "Fasten the back of this for me, will you?"

"Now, wait a minute..." I began.

"I don't have to let you stay here. I can call Gus and have you thrown out. I'm only letting you stay out of the goodness of my heart. Now, fasten this for me." She smiled. "Please."

I reached inside her robe and fastened the belt in the back.

"Thanks."

"I don't know what you've got to do with this, Gail. I think you got yourself mixed up in rough company, too rough. But I think inside you're decent, you've got a heart. I don't think you'd go as far as letting a girl be killed when you could save her life by telling me where Pete has taken her."

She sat down again, and poured a shot out of a bottle that was on the dressing table. "Want a drink?"

I shook my head.

"What's your name? Funny, I've been thinking about you all day and I don't even know your name."

"John," I said.

"Johnny." She said the name not to me but to the air, testing the sound of it. "I told them that they were nuts, that you weren't no cop or federal agent or whatever the hell you are. You know what I told them? I told them you were a nice guy." She laughed. "Maybe you are, at that."

"Listen to me. There's a chance for you. You're mixed up in a spy ring that's over your head. It's bigger than you think. It means thousands of lives. You're a traitor to your country, do you know that?"

She didn't answer.

"The game is up. We're wise to all of you now. Charlie is dead." I waited for a reaction. There didn't seem to be any. "Did you hear what I said? Charlie's dead."

"Okay, so he's dead. I'm not sorry. I won't have to feel those greasy yellow fingers pawing me anymore. I'm glad he's dead."

"The rest of you will be caught. Tonight. It's over. Do you understand what I'm saying? It's over, your spy ring is through."

She picked up a nail file and began on her nails. "So it's over. So everything is over. What the hell do I care?"

"If you tell me where Pete took the girl, if you talk about who else is in this with you, I can see that you get off easy. Look, baby, I know a lot about you. I know that you're not in this to destroy this country, the way Charlie and Polyton and the rest of them are. You're in because of the dough and the feeling of security the dough gives you. You're a dumb blonde but you've got a heart that's as big as the rest of you. If you were smarter, you'd have realized just how dangerous this spy operation is. You would have realized how much harm you were doing your own country. If you were smarter you wouldn't be mixed up in this. If you tell me what I want to know, I'll see that you get off easy. I'll go to bat for you and explain what makes you tick, what made you get mixed up with foreign agents. I'll tell them that at the zero hour you wised up and worked on our side, worked for me. How about it?"

"And if I don't?"

"You'll die like the rest of them."

"I told Charlie that you were a sweet guy, that you weren't part of no counterspy system. You are a sweet guy, Johnny. You're understanding, you're—Oh, what's the difference? It's too late now."

"Is the girl dead?"

"I don't know. I honest-to-God don't know. We had a fight, me and Charlie. I said I was through, I wouldn't have no more to do with it. I tried to pull out." She turned to me and there were real tears sticking in the fake eyelashes. "Cross my heart, Johnny, I tried to get out. It hit me all of a sudden what we were doing. I wanted out before anything else happened."

"Well?"

She dropped the robe from her shoulders. There were four fresh red whip marks on her back. "Pete had some fun. There's no getting out."

"Do you swear to God that you don't know where Pete took the girl?"

Her voice was soft-sounding, the way words are spoken in a confessional. "I swear I don't know. I swear it to God."

"Have you got any ideas? You must have heard something about the plan."

"Nothing. I didn't hear nothing. He won't kill her quick, that's all I know. Pete, he takes his time. It's like going to bed for him, beating up some dame and killing her. He gets his kicks that way. He'll make it last a long time before she's dead."

"Now, listen to me, Gail, and listen carefully. There is a big boss of this spy ring. You know who that is, don't you?"

Her back was to me but she looked at me through the mirror, frightened. She dropped her head into her arms and began to cry.

"I know who it is too, Gail, but I've got to have proof. You've got to give me that proof."

She didn't raise her head or make any effort to say anything.

"You admitted you made a mistake getting mixed up in this. Give me the evidence I need and you'll have every possible protection. I'll do everything in my power to see that you get a break in the trial. If you testify against this person, the jury will go easy on you. What about it?"

"I'm scared," she murmured.

"You don't have to be scared, believe me. Right now, I want you to write it out, write down that you know who the chief of this spy system is, write down his name and sign it. I'll dictate it to you. I need that evidence." I pulled my fountain pen out of my pocket. There was a letter from an insurance company in my wallet. The back of it was good enough to use to write out her confession. "Here, take these. Please. Take these and write down what I tell you. Here." I held the pen and paper out to her.

For a minute she didn't move. Then, slowly, she raised her head and turned to me. She was smiling. I knew that it was all right now, that she was going to do as I asked her.

But as she reached for the pen, the smile left her face. Fear made her eyes wide. She screamed, "Look out, Johnny! Look out!" In the second of the scream, using all her weight and power, the big blonde stood up and shoved my chair, and I fell off, flat on the floor. The light went out in that same split second and two shots flared across the room. Glass shattered. The mirror over the dressing table had been hit.

The door slammed. The gunman was gone. I had drawn my gun but I didn't even bother to go after him. I groped around the floor. My hand touched the big blonde. She didn't move. I put my hand to her chest. It was silent, made still by the clean cuttings of the bullet. And where my hand touched the lifeless flesh, it touched the warm, sticky liquid of blood.

CHAPTER TWELVE

The backstage corridor was empty when I stepped out of the blonde's dressing room seconds later. Up front the show was still going on. The gunshots had not been heard. I walked cautiously toward the stage. Gradually, I became aware of the music that was being played. It was the music for the slave dance, Gail's dance. I passed the tinny orchestra playing behind the curtain and stumbled on a strange bent-over man playing the lute, plucking the strings with shaking fingers.

Then I heard it, the cracking sound of the whip.

Pete!

The scream of a girl followed the sound of the whip.

I ran and stood in the wings. Pete was on the stage, his long, gold-glittering body leaping with orgiastic fervor.

Where Gail usually stood, a post had been placed. Tied to the post, half-naked and screaming, was Chloe. Already there were two red slashes of the whip across her thighs.

The stage manager was standing near me. I drew my gun and thrust it in his back. "Do as I say and you won't be hurt." He started to turn his head but I pressed the gun harder to him. "Drop the curtain," I commanded. "Drop it." He pulled a cord and the asbestos curtain came down abruptly. The dancers stopped but the offstage music continued.

Using the stage manager as a shield, I walked on stage. "Now, none of you move and nothing will happen," I said.

I said to the stage manager, "Untie the girl."

"Look, mister," he said, "I didn't know nothing about this. Pete said Gail wasn't feeling good and this was a new—"

I jabbed the gun at him. "Never mind what Pete said. Untie her."

Meanwhile, panting heavily, Pete stood stage center holding the whip. He was all animal now, not human. He was all unsatisfied animal, trapped and glowering, poised and waiting to spring out of the trap. I kept my eye sharp on him, ready for the first move.

The cast was silent, frightened. Out front there was a lot of noise, clapping and stamping of feet, calls of "More! More!" Chloe passed out and slumped to the floor as soon as she was untied. It was going to make it more difficult to get out of there if I had to carry her. And I had to move fast. The killer who had aimed at me and hit the big blonde might still be in the place. I knew that this time he wouldn't miss.

Keeping the gun steady, with my left arm I pulled down one of the purple curtains decorating the stage. I held it out to the stage manager. "Put this around her," I said.

Chloe came back to consciousness when he wrapped the purple curtain tight about her. She stood up and staggered over to me. "Johnny, Johnny, I thought it was all over."

"Stay behind me," I said. "We're going to back out of here. Look out in the back to make sure no one tries to stop us."

I kept watching Pete as we moved backward. He was desperate, I knew that, and he was thinking with animal instinctiveness and sensitivity. Every muscle of his body showed through the thin covering of gold paint. They were muscles of a tiger about to spring on his victim, quivering with the power being exerted to hold those muscles in check until the moment for the kill came.

He leaped fast. My shot missed him and the tip of his whip lashed my hand and my gun fell away. I pushed Chloe to the floor and headed for him.

The whip came across my arm but I kept moving toward him, sailing into him with a football tackle. The people on stage screamed and yelled. The noise now was almost deafening. There was no time for thinking, there wasn't time to be smart. This was kill or be killed.

I hung on him, not letting him back away far enough to get leverage to swing that whip. The coating of gold paint made him slippery, hard to hold onto. We fell over and I had the ballet dancer nailed to the floor. He was powerful in his struggle to get free, writhing and wiggling around like a snake. But I held fast, pressing as hard as I could on the hand that held the whip. After a couple of minutes of intense pressure it was too much for him and his grip gave way and the whip fell free. I kicked it out of reach.

"Okay," I said. "Now how tough do you feel without your whip?"

He didn't answer. He didn't have to. He was still tough enough to be giving me a whale of a workout. I was a better match for him this time. We were landing punches pretty evenly. It was funny the way he fought. It was more than fighting for him; each blow he landed gave him great sensual pleasure. And he took the blows the same way, his body sucking in the force of my fist, enjoying the sensation of the hurting. In clinches, he pressed me against him some of the time, beginning almost as a gesture of love and turning into vicious pressure and hurting blows.

It seemed as though the fight lasted for a long, long time. In actual minutes, I don't know how long it was.

There was one punch, a hell of a solid blow to my face, that sent me stumbling backward across the stage. There were screams of women as I fell back. I blanked out for a minute when I hit the floor. When my eyes opened, I saw him coming toward me again. He had retrieved the whip and was about to let loose with it. I put my arm up over my face, automatically, instinctively self-protective.

A gun fired. I lowered my arm. The ballet dancer slowed up, his body straightened and stiffened for a second, and then he slumped to the floor. I watched him, not believing what I was seeing. Then I looked past him, toward the edge of the stage.

Chloe still had the gun in her hand. She held it steadily, not quivering. I ran over to her.

Her voice was low, shaking under the veneer of calm. "Take the gun, Johnny. Take it. Please take it."

I tried to take the gun from her but her muscles had frozen tight around it and I had to pry it away.

"Is he dead, Johnny?"

I looked at the body. There seemed to be no movement from it. I shouted to the stage manager. "You. See if he's breathing."

The people on the stage had become silent. They were watching this as though it were a play and they were the audience. The stage manager leaned over the gilded body of the ballet dancer and listened over his heart. "I can't hear nothing," he said.

Chloe whispered, "I killed him. I killed him."

"Steady, baby. Steady."

"Let's get out of here, Johnny. Please. Please let's get out of here before something else happens."

"You didn't have to do it," I said. "I was handling him all right. I would have taken care of him."

"It was there," she said. "Your gun was there on the floor. I would have done it sooner. I saw it but I couldn't seem to move. I don't know what was holding me. But when he picked up the whip, I did it without thinking about what I was doing. I did it because I had to do it."

I put my arm around her and held her close to me. "It's all right, Chloe. It's all over now."

"I'm not sorry, Johnny. He had it coming. He was—he was awful, Johnny. Terrible. Awful. I can't begin to—"

"Don't say anything else. It's over. He can't hurt you."

Outside, I heard the sirens coming. Someone had called the police. I couldn't let them catch me. There was no time to go through the channels to explain to the police what I was doing. My job was still not finished. I couldn't get caught up in the red tape of an arrest.

We got out through the side door of the Keyhole. It led out to an alley. We started running toward the street at the far end of it. Chloe was barefoot, and the debris-littered pavement was rough on her feet. She didn't say anything, kept moving like a soldier, but I could tell she was suffering. I picked her up and carried her.

At the street I looked down toward the entrance of the club. A whole line of squad cars was there and the police were just getting out. A taxi came by and I hailed it, but there was a radio-dispatched cab coming down the street behind it, so I let the first cab go by and we got into the second one. I had an idea.

"Where to, folks?"

"Start driving," I said. "Anywhere."

He turned around smiling. He saw Chloe wrapped in the purple curtain from the stage. "So that's what this is all about! They're pulling a raid on the Chinese Keyhole. You in the show, miss?"

Chloe looked at me. "Yes." I said. "She's in the show. She's a stripper. We're both in the show. We got two kids. We don't want our names in the newspaper. We don't want the kids to know. That's why we've got to get away so fast."

He pulled the flag and started to drive. "I may be obstructing justice," he said. "It may be I ought to turn you in."

"Look, pal, I told you we've got two kids. They've got to eat and wear clothes. This is the way we make a living. Like you drive your hack. It's what you know how to do and this is what we know how to do."

"Okay, so I don't turn you in. I got three kids. Driving a hack is cleaner work. Of course, my missus ain't as good-looking as yours. Otherwise, who knows?" He turned back and smiled at us. "You don't care where I drive?"

"No, anywhere." The radio in the front seat was making a lot of noise, calls going through to other cabs. "Turn that down, will you, driver?"

"I got to listen in case I get a call."

"Radio your dispatch station that you've got a load going for a long ride and that you'll contact them later."

"They're going to think it's funny."

"I don't care what they think. Go ahead. Please," I added.

He switched on his set. "This is Cab Forty-eight. Mike?"

A voice came through the speaker. "Cab Forty-eight. Go ahead."

"Mike, I got a load going for a long ride. I can't take no calls for a while. Okay?"

"Cab Forty-eight. Okay, radio in when you're through. And Al, I got something to tell you. Esperito knocked out Modaluski in the fifth. You owe me a sawbuck." He laughed. "See you later, Al."

The driver turned the volume almost all the way down. "What do you know?" he said. "It's the first fight Modaluski has lost this year. And it's the one fight I had money on him."

We waited until we were a good distance away from the Keyhole, then both Chloe and I relaxed. "What are we going to do, Johnny?"

"I'm not sure yet. You're still in danger."

"Still in danger?"

"Yes. The big man is still at large. I don't know what he's going to do next. I can't take a chance with you again. You're not safe until he's caught."

"What about you? You're not safe either."

I laughed. "I'm never safe, baby. Never."

"You know who it is, don't you?"

"Yes. It took me too long to find out, but I know now."

"Will you tell me?"

I shook my head. "No. Not yet. It would only put you in more danger if you knew."

"How did you find out who it is? Was it something I said, I mean when I told about all the people who came to see Polyton?"

"It was partly that. It was a lot of things that fitted together very suddenly, very surprisingly. You helped. You helped a lot. I was sent into an ambush, a trap. But that could have been a couple of people's fault. But when I found that you had been kidnaped from the hotel, I was sure, I was positive. There's only one person who could have known you were there."

"Are you going to take him into custody right away?"

"There's a question of proof. I know he's the man, but I can't prove it. And the people who could prove it are dead. Pete, Charlie Moy, Gail. No witnesses."

Chloe snuggled in closer to me. I took her hand and held it tight. "What about Polyton, Johnny? He could tell, couldn't he? He must know."

"He's my only chance. If he's still alive."

"What do you mean?"

"We know that Polyton is the only one who can put the finger on the big boss. And one other person knows that—the big boss himself. Polyton is too dangerous for him to leave alive."

"I know where he lives. There may still be time."

"I could find the man and shoot him down," I said. "It's the way he works. He shoots from behind. He did it to a sweet guy named Tom White. He tried to do it to me. I could shoot him down. There wouldn't have to be witnesses or evidence against him. It would be murder. Justifiable murder, maybe. Eliminating the danger." I paused, thinking. "You want to know something?"

"What?"

"I could murder him. That's what it would be. I could murder him and no one would ever touch me. I'm an agent and I could get away with it in the line of duty. But I don't think I'd ever be the same man again. I'd be like him, the same kind of unscrupulous coward."

"You forget, Johnny. I killed a man tonight. From behind, the way you said. I shot him when he wasn't looking. But I feel clean about it. To kill a man is a horrible thing, but ..."

"You had cause, Chloe. You had lots of reasons. There was what he did to you. That was reason enough. And there was what he was going to do to me. I didn't thank you, did I, for saving my life?"

"I didn't save your life, Johnny. You were handling him just fine. You were really beating him up, but—well, this was quicker."

I laughed and took her hand again. "I don't think so, Chloe. I think I was on the losing end of that fight. Thanks. If not for my life, at least I can thank you for saving me from getting messed up by that whip."

For the next few blocks we were silent again. Then Chloe said, "What have you decided to do, Johnny?"

"I better do it right. Where does Polyton live?"

She gave me the address and I repeated it to the driver. "I went up there one night," she said. "He had a party for the whole office staff. He and his wife. She's such a cute old lady. A little bit of a thing with white hair. I wonder if she knows that her husband is a traitor."

"Probably not," I said.

"What's the matter, Maguire? What's wrong with you? You're so quiet and unenthusiastic. You had so much fire about this thing before. You've been going after this case as though it were important to you. Now you're so close to the end of it and you're not excited anymore."

"I know. I don't like what I'm going to have to do."

"You mean the boss of the spy ring?"

I nodded. "It's funny how wrong you can be about a guy. And now, when I should be remembering all the horrible things he's done, I'm sitting here remembering nice things about him, the things that made me like him."

"He's a friend?"

"I don't know whether you say was or is. He tried to kill me an hour ago. I suppose you would say was."

"Except that you're still fond of him."

"I suppose so. It sounds like such a dumb thing to be saying about a man I should hate so. When I don't think about who he is, if I could just concentrate on what he has done, what he stands for, the danger he is to the world, then I could hate him. I could hate him enough to murder him, shoot him down without warning or without thinking twice. But I keep remembering that besides being a spy, he's also a man. In some ways, we're very much alike. We've had fun together."

"You are a funny man, Maguire. You're such a choirboy inside all that gruffness. Incidentally, I never thanked you."

"For what?"

"For keeping a promise to me. This afternoon, in the hotel, when I wanted you so badly, you said that I would have another chance to live. You said that—"

I stopped her. "We said a lot of things this afternoon."

"We talked about love, didn't we?"

"Yes, I guess we did."

"Do you want to talk about it again?"

"Not now. Not yet."

"All right, Johnny. I can wait."

I leaned forward to the driver. "Step it up a little more, will you?"

"No need, Mac. You're here."

There were two police cars and an ambulance in front of Polyton's house. I wasn't surprised. I knew that it would have to be that way. The killer had gone from the Keyhole to get rid of Polyton. It was the logical move, an inevitable outcome.

"Driver, stop a minute."

The front door of the house was open and two orderlies carried out a stretcher, a sheet completely covering the body. A little old lady walked beside the corpse, hovering over the stretcher, touching the dead remnants of the man she had loved.

"All right, driver, move on. Head back toward the north side."

"Say, mister, I can't help hearing what you been saying back there. I know that hackers are supposed to be deaf to any conversation, but I don't understand what's going on. I mean, first I pick you up and you say you're one thing. Then you give me an address and we get there and they're carrying out a stiff."

"I'll tell you what I'll do, pal. When this is all over, we'll get together over a couple of beers and I'll tell you the whole story. Okay?"

He didn't answer. I looked down at Chloe. She was crying.

"I feel so sorry for that old lady," she said. "You knew that it was going to happen, didn't you? That's why you didn't hurry or weren't excited. You knew that Polyton would be killed, didn't you?"

"Yes, I knew. I couldn't have stopped it. No matter what, I would have been too late."

"Now what?"

"I'm on my own, I guess. I've got to do it my own way. There isn't anyone to give evidence now. Except me. And I have to get it."

"Be careful, Johnny. Don't let anything happen to you. There's so much that I haven't told you. I've grown up a million years since this afternoon."

"I'll be all right." I leaned forward again and spoke to the driver. "I'm going to get off in a few more blocks. You keep driving with the lady, will you? I'm leaving her in your charge. When there is no more danger I'll phone your office downtown and they'll radio an address for you to bring her to. Here's twenty bucks, and there'll be another twenty for you at the end of the line."

"Tell them to radio Cab Number Forty-eight."

"I'll remember. Pull up on the next corner."

Chloe said, "I know that you're going to do this your own way, Johnny. Nothing I say will be any use, will it?"

"This is more than a job, Chloe. There are a lot of personal things mixed up in it."

"Just be careful, Johnny. Don't let anything happen to you."

I kissed her long and hard. The kiss was an action complete in itself. It said what there was to say between Chloe and me. And it said what I was feeling inside. It said that maybe this was the last girl I would ever kiss. It was every kiss I had ever kissed and every kiss I had ever wanted to kiss. It was long and hard. That kind of kiss.

The cab had stopped. I got out quickly, without a word. I signaled the driver and he started off.

The storm that had been threatening had not come to be. The night had cleared and it was warm. Above the tall buildings I watched the stars. I was seeing them as a lover sees them and I was seeing them as a scientist studies them. At that moment, I was many men with many wishes.

I began to whistle a tune, a nameless melody.

Then slowly, easily, I started to walk toward my apartment.

CHAPTER THIRTEEN

The darkness of my apartment there was one spot of light, the burning end of a cigarette. There was the gentle clink of the brandy bottle against a glass.

"Hello, Jacques."

"Hello, Johnny."

"I wasn't sure you'd be here, yet."

"Yet? I have not left," he said.

When I flicked on the light his eyes didn't squint. It meant he hadn't been in the darkness there very long. "What's new, Frenchie?"

He shrugged his shoulders. "There is nothing." He motioned to the brandy bottle. "Drink?" He smiled then. "I am being most generous with your brandy, no?"

I picked up the bottle. He hadn't had time to make much of a dent in it. "I don't know, you're taking it pretty easy tonight. I expected you'd have half the bottle killed by now." He filled a glass for me. I sat down near him on the davenport and took the glass.

"*A votre santé,* Johnny."

"Yeah. Mud in your eye." I swallowed it quickly.

"You Americans, you do everything so quick. You must drink the brandy slowly. Hold the glass in your hand like so, to warm it. You must treat it with a loving hand, like the brandy it is a woman you love."

"I'll remember that."

He filled my glass again. This time I cupped the glass in my hand and held it tightly.

"How did it go, Johnny? I see the way your clothes are. There has been a fight, no?"

"Lots of fights, Jacques. Plenty of trouble."

"You got what you were after?"

"Sure. Sure. I got what I was after."

He switched his position. "You found him, this man you were hunting?"

"Yes. I found him."

"It was rough?"

"Rough," I said. "Very rough. Too many people were killed. And there's one more to go."

"This man, this head of the spy ring, you have no doubt that it is the right man?"

I looked at him straight. "No, Jacques. I have no doubt at all."

"Then I congratulate you. I also drink to you." This time he was the one who downed his brandy in one gulp. "I am also sorry that it has to be this way."

"What way, Jacques? What way is it?"

His hand had been resting between the seat cushions of the davenport. He raised it now. There was a gun in it and it was pointing at me.

I laughed a little. "You won't shoot me, Jacques."

"It's a thing I most deeply regret, but it is also a thing I will have to do."

He leaned forward and started to reach inside my coat. I drew back.

"Do not move, please," he said. "I want your gun. I do not think I can trust you to have the gun on your person."

"I'll give it to you."

"Oh, no, Johnny. I would not put you to the trouble." He pulled my gun out of the holster and put it in his pocket.

"You know, Jacques, I walked a long time tonight. Just now, I mean. I walked a long way home because I wanted to have time to think. About you, mostly."

"You are thinking how clever he is, this Jacques? How he has fooled so many people for so long?"

"Not that, really. You were clever, Jacques. Up to a point. I don't know when I became suspicious of you for the first time. Maybe it was in my mind for a long time before I realized it. Maybe I didn't want to see the evidence against you, Jacques, because you were my friend. When I walked into the trap at Moy's house I was pretty sure. When I got to the hotel and found that Chloe had been kidnaped I was positive. There were only three people who knew where Chloe was. You and Chloe and me."

"I did not expect you to get out of the trap at Moy's house. Under equal circumstances, I would not give a thousand Charlie Moys for one John Maguire. But in this circumstance Moy had the advantage, he had time and surprise in his favor. You must have been more brilliant than usual to outwit him."

"I was brilliant as hell, Jacques." I reached into my pocket for a cigarette, and my fingers closed around my pocketknife. My technique was a little rusty, but I managed to get it out of my pocket along with the cigarettes and up my sleeve without Jacques's noticing it. The problem then was to get him in position so that I could let him have it without getting it myself.

Jacques had jumped up and raised his gun when he saw my hand go into my pocket.

"Only a cigarette, Jacques," I said. "I wouldn't try to outdraw you, even if I had another gun, which I don't."

He smiled. "A pity. It would make it easier for me if you would try something. It would be self-defense, is it not?"

I managed to laugh. "You know, we're a lot alike, Jacques. I was wondering too about how I would kill you when I found you. It's hard to shoot down a man in cold blood. Even a man I hate as much as you."

"You do not hate me, Johnny. You do not hate Jacques Marples. You hate this man who is a spy against your country. You hate this man who has killed your friend Tom White."

"You're wrong, Frenchie. It isn't just what you've done, it's what you are that I hate, too. I didn't think so at first. When I realized that you were the man I've been after for so long, it hit me hard. You were my friend. I didn't have to walk in here, Jacques. I knew you would be sitting where you were. I could have done it another way. I could have shot you immediately, before you had a chance to use your gun. I was a sap, I suppose, not to. It would have been my job to do it that way."

He stood up, over me, the nose of the gun close to my head. "Then you should have done it. If you knew I was here and you knew I was the man you were after, it was your job to shoot me. Regardless of anything else, you should have shot me."

I kept my voice calm and casual. I was taking time, waiting for my chance. "I thought about doing it that way. I thought I should just sneak up behind you somewhere and let you have six shots. Five for the five you put in Tom White, and one for a girl named Leona who loved him. I promised her that. I promised her that one slug I put in you would be from her."

"Speaking of girls, Johnny, this Chloe …" He hesitated.

"What about her?"

"I think you had better tell me where she is."

"What for?"

He shrugged his shoulders. "It is another precaution. I am thinking that perhaps you have told her about me."

It was an opportunity and I grabbed it. "You've been wondering, haven't you, Jacques, why I'm being so calm? I mean, let's be realistic about this thing. The fact that we were once friends doesn't make any difference now. There's no sentiment between us any more, is there?"

"It is unfortunate, but it is true."

"You've got a gun on me but I'm sitting here quietly, not rattled. I'm not even worried about dying. Because regardless of what you do to me, Jacques, you're through. Chloe knows the whole story. She knows about the trunk at Moy's place and she knows that you're the key man Biget is after. She knows everything that you and I know. And one other thing. She knows how to contact Biget." I looked at my watch. As I raised my hand I felt the knife glide along my arm. "According to my timetable, she ought to be in contact with Biget by now."

The smile went off his face. He twisted nervously, then forced the smile to come back. "How do you call it, Johnny—the bluff?"

"It's no bluff, Jacques."

"Where is this girl?"

I mocked his gesture and shrugged my shoulders. "*Qui sait,* Jacques? Anywhere."

He stood up. "You will tell me where you have hidden the girl."

"You know me better than that. I won't talk."

"You love her. That is it, is it not?"

"It's got nothing to do with anything. Whether I love her or not doesn't matter."

"It matters very greatly. Do you love her enough so that you would die to save her?"

I let the knife slip down so that it was in my hand again. Holding my hand hidden against my leg, I released the blade. "Are you trying to offer me a trade, my life for hers?"

He thought for a moment. "Yes."

I laughed and sat forward on the couch. My head was level with his waist. I figured that if I could buck him and slide under him, even if he fired the gun, there was a good chance the shot would miss me; I would be too close. "I don't believe you, Jacques. You wouldn't trade anything. You can't let either of us live. Not and stay alive yourself. The hell with getting proof and getting evidence. You know we'll get you."

"Tell me, where is the girl? Tell me. Quickly! Quickly!"

I feigned a move backward with my head and then reversed quickly and bucked him hard in the stomach, pushing forward so that when he fell I fell under him. The gun discharged, explosive shots in the empty softness of the davenport upholstery. Almost with the same gesture the knife went into his chest. Because he was partially on top of me, I didn't have leverage to make more than one thrust. But the one stab was enough to slow him up and give me a chance to grab my gun, which he had put in his pocket. I scrambled to my feet and Jacques rolled over with his gun pointing at me. I shot at his arm and his gun fired a misdirected shot and fell out of his hand.

Blood came freely from around the knife, which was still in his chest, and his arm bled badly too. He lay back on the floor, his energy spent, his breathing heavy. "You were right," he said. The words came out in a gruff whisper, labored words that were hard to say. "I was not smart enough for you, Johnny. I am glad for this one thing." He coughed a little. I didn't move. "I am glad that it is you who have done this to me. You are like me, Johnny. It is most unfortunate that we are on the different sides. I could not have died happy if someone unworthy had tricked me. Like this Tom White, this stupid dolt of a man. It is now that I die with honor for my country and for the cause for which I fight."

"You're not dying, Jacques, and you know it." The knife wound was below his heart and the bullet in his arm may have been painful but it wasn't fatal. Neither of the wounds was.

Jacques shook his head. "I will not leave this room alive. You know that."

"Yes, you will. I'm not going to shoot you now. I should, maybe, to make up for Tom White. But I think maybe Biget will have some questions to ask you. He'll want to know lots of things."

"There will never be a chance." He raised himself up on his elbow.

"Stay where you are, Jacques."

He kept moving and was in a sitting position. "Why don't you shoot, Johnny?"

I didn't say anything, I just watched him get to his feet. "Well, Johnny?"

"Sit down on the couch."

He smiled at me. "You must not be sentimental. I admit it, I was. I should have shot you the moment you were inside that door. Do not make my mistake, Johnny. Do not be sentimental."

"Sentiment, hell. You didn't shoot me because you wanted to make me tell you where Chloe is. Dying fast is too good for you. You ought to be made to suffer."

He took a few steps toward the door. "Stop, Jacques." He kept moving. I fired and winked him in the shoulder. He stopped, straightened up with pain, then fell to the floor. In the silence, I stood motionless, waiting. He turned his head toward me. "Two, Johnny. Two shots. Three more to go." He tried to laugh. "Four. I forget the girl."

Again he was able to raise himself up. He stumbled toward the door.

"Jacques, I'm warning you."

He shook his head. "It hurts now, Johnny. Shoot through. Finish the job. Please. Please." He kept walking until his hand was on the doorknob. I fired again. I don't know where he got the strength. He had the door partially opened. There was nothing else to do. I fired the remaining shots and he slumped to the floor. This time, I knew it was forever.

When I rolled the body over, the eyes were open and there was a smile across the dead lips. I took the knife out of his chest, wiped the blade clean on my handkerchief, and put it back into my pocket.

There was noise outside the apartment door. I pulled the body forward and opened the door. There were several people out there. I didn't bother to try to recognize their faces. "There's been an accident," I said. "I've called the police. Go away, please. Everything has been taken care of." I slammed the door.

I went into the bedroom, picked up the phone, and slowly dialed the number that Biget had given me.

Jenkins' voice answered.

I said, "Biget."

"Maguire?"

"Yes."

"Did you get him?"

"Yes."

"Dead or alive?"

"Dead," I said. "He's here. In my apartment."

"Who is it, Maguire?"

I started to say his name but it wouldn't come out. It was choked up somewhere inside me.

"Are you all right, Maguire?"

"Yeah, I'm fine. Come and get him." I hung up. Then I called the number of the taxicab company and said, "Make contact with Cab Number Forty-eight. Tell him to pick me up in front of Sixty Briargate."

In the bathroom, I washed my face and hands, combed my hair, then changed clothes. The slug that had been taken from Tom White's back was in the pocket of the suit I had been wearing. I started to transfer it to the other suit, then changed my mind and tossed it into the wastebasket. I listened for a moment to the thick, dead sound it made as it landed.

The tie, the coded one that Jacques had given me the night before, lay where I had thrown it on a chair. I put it on.

On my way out, I stood for a moment over Jacques. There was nothing to do and there was nothing to say. Yet unspoken words were running a circle in my head. God forgive me, they were saying. God forgive me.

I pulled down my hat and went outside to wait for Chloe.

CHAPTER FOURTEEN

While I was standing downstairs waiting for the taxi, a big car pulled up in front of the building. One of the four men who got out was Colonel Jenkins. I stayed where I was and he came up to me.

"I left the door open. Apartment Three A."

"Nice work, Maguire. You did a good job and you did it fast."

"There's a trunk load of machinery parts and blueprints." I gave him Moy's address and the keys to the trunk. "They were going to be shipped out of the country tomorrow. Or maybe it's today. Is it midnight?" I checked my watch. "Yes," I said, "they were going to be shipped out today."

"Washington is going to know the kind of job you did. There will be a promotion for you."

"And more dough?"

"Yes, Johnny, more dough."

"Do you know who you're going to find up there, Colonel?"

He shook his head.

"Jacques Marples."

He still didn't say anything.

"Are you surprised?"

"In this business, Maguire, there are no surprises," Jenkins said. "I wouldn't have been surprised if it had been the girl from Iowa."

Just then the taxi pulled up. Chloe's head was at the window, searching anxiously. When she saw me, she smiled and sat back. "No, the girl from Iowa is all right," I said.

"Incidentally, Maguire, we're even."

"What do you mean?"

"You just saved my neck by licking this case for me. Washington had me on the carpet. It was crack this spy ring, or else."

I laughed. "We're not even. I saved your job maybe, but you saved my life."

"Doing what I'm doing, Johnny, is my life." He gave me a light sock on the shoulder, motioned to his men, and went into the building.

I walked over and got into the cab beside Chloe.

She looked me over carefully, running her fingers over my face, down my arms, across my chest. "You're all right."

I slumped down in the seat. "Yeah, I'm just nifty."

The driver had turned around and was grinning at me. "Me and your girlfriend had a nice ride. We went down by the planetarium, we rode along the lake. My wife will never believe this."

"Take us to College Drive." I turned to Chloe. "We'll go to your place."

He started away and I lighted a cigarette.

"Do you feel like talking, Johnny?"

I started to say no, and then stopped, because to my surprise I suddenly realized it wasn't true. For a long time I had thought of Jacques Marples as my friend, and I had just killed him, and Chloe knew nothing about it. But she would know soon enough, and all at once it was important that she should understand how it had been.

"You remember the Frenchman who came to see Polyton?" I said. "The Charles Boyer type?"

"Yes," she said. "Jacques Marples. Your friend."

"No!" I said harshly. "He was not my friend. I thought he was, but I was wrong. He never was my friend." I forced my voice to become more gentle. "That's what I've got to get through my thick head. Because he was the one, Chloe. He was the one behind this whole rotten mess. He was the one who killed Tom White. And I just killed him."

"Oh, Johnny!" She took my hand in both of hers. We were silent for a few seconds. Then, "Johnny? If he was the head of the spy ring, how did he make you think he was on our side?"

"Oh, he was on our side, all right. He was my contact with Biget. You didn't know that, did you? He was damn clever. There's no better place to be than right in the middle, working for both sides. He knew all along how close we were to breaking up his spy ring. He could be as brazen as he wanted when he knew we were way off the track. And when we got hot on the trail he could pull in his horns and lie low for a while."

"Yes," she said quietly, "that was clever. But he wasn't clever enough to get away with it. You found out about him. How did you, Johnny?"

"He was the one who sent me into the trap at Moy's house, and he was the only person besides you and me who knew you were at the Payton Hotel this afternoon. I had told him, you see. It had to be him. And it was. He admitted it just before I—I killed him."

"Oh, Johnny, I'm so dreadfully sorry it had to be that way. I know how you must feel."

"No, it's all right, Chloe," I said, and by that time it was. "I'm not sorry he's dead. He was a killer, and he was doing his damnedest to sell this country out to the Reds. That's the part that's hard to understand. Because at one time he really was on our side, and he did his damnedest for us, too. That was in France, during the war. He was with the French underground, and he did a hell of a job for them. I worked with him there, and I know. He risked his neck every day of his life during the war. On our side."

Chloe let go of my hand and leaned forward, her eyes wide and puzzled. "But if he risked his life, he must have believed in what he was fighting for. What did he think it was, anyway?"

"I suppose it sounds corny, but it's the thing I was fighting for too, I guess. In those days we were both fighting for the same thing. Freedom."

"But the side he was fighting for now is the opposite of all that. How could he switch sides so easily?"

"I don't think he did switch easily," I said slowly. "It's a little hard to understand, but I knew him well enough to know that he wasn't just a professional killer, or a guy out for the main chance. He wouldn't work for the Reds just for what it paid him. He wasn't that kind of guy. The morals and the politics behind it must have had some meaning for him."

Chloe said nothing, and I leaned back in the seat, trying to figure out what had happened to this man who had been my friend. Because I was wrong; Jacques *had* been my friend, back in France, when we had both been willing to die for the same thing.

"I suppose," I said finally, "it boils down to the fact that during the war I was fighting to keep something I already had, and Jacques was fighting to get something he had been promised but never had had, and never did get. In this country we really know what peace is. We've lived freely and we've never been invaded and bombed. But in France it seems as if they've known nothing but war. This last war was supposed to give them peace at last. They thought the United States would give it to them. Hell, we told them so ourselves. And they believed it. Jacques believed it so strongly he risked his life for it."

"But how could they expect us to give them those things?" Chloe broke in angrily. "It's not—"

"Easy," I said. "I'm just trying to say what I think Jacques believed. Maybe it's not important, anyway. The important thing was to get rid of the Germans. This time for good. When they were gone, France would be free and prosperous, like the United States. Only it didn't turn out that way. They traded the Germans for the Americans, and France is still poor. Those who grew rich with the Germans have grown richer with the Americans. And so they no longer think that we have the answer."

"Yes," Chloe said. "I guess it's understandable. Jacques turned away from us, and there were the Communists. He thought maybe they had the answer."

Neither of us said anything more for several moments, and then Chloe stirred and reached for my hand again. She let out a little sigh before she spoke.

"Johnny, do you like the sound of my voice?"

"Huh? Sure I do. You've got a nice voice."

"That's good," she said, "because I want to talk now. I want to forget about Jacques Marples and talk to you. About you and me."

"What about us?"

"We drove for a long time. Al and me. I had a long time for thinking. I didn't know whether you would ever call for me. I knew that you were walking into danger. I made a pact with myself. If you were killed … I'm not being silly about this. I mean there was that possibility, wasn't there?"

"Me?" I said. "Hell, I'm indestructible."

"Well, I decided that if anything happened to you tonight, I was going to go on with this work. Being a spy, I mean. And I decided something else, too. I mean what I was going to do if anything happened to you. You know what I decided?" She paused to catch her breath, not to hear an answer. "I decided that the next time I fell in love or—well, wanted someone the way I wanted you—I would go through with it. Regardless of anything."

I laughed. "Lucky I didn't get killed, isn't it? I saved you from living a life of sin."

"I'm serious, Johnny. You're teasing me and I'm being very serious. You see, I've grown up since yesterday. Really, I have. I thought I was grown-up before; I had a career, I was doing important work, I was living alone, I was being terribly independent. But it wasn't being grown-up. I was lonely, incomplete. Do I make any sense at all?"

"Sure, you make a lot of sense. All these things you were doing, you were doing because you were mad, because a guy you thought you loved was killed in the war. I'm not saying anything against what you were doing, because it was fine and noble. It was good work for a good cause. I'm talking about the reasons for it. I suppose if you were really grown-up, you would have got over the guy who was killed, found another guy, and lived a normal life in Nebraska or Iowa or wherever the hell it is."

"You're making it easier for me to say the other thing. I mean the other alternative of what I would do if you weren't killed, if nothing happened to you."

"You don't have to say it, little one. I know. You want to go home, don't you? Back to the guy in Nebraska."

She didn't say anything. I looked over at her. She was crying a little, dribbly tears, and nodding. "Yes, Johnny, I want to go home and I want the boy from Nebraska."

"Go ahead, Chloe, take it while you can get it."

"I still love you, Johnny. I know it must sound just dreadful to say I love one man and want to marry another. I love him, too, but it's different. I know it wouldn't last with us, would it? I mean, I was thinking that maybe we were in love with each other because of the danger. We were kind of pushed together, forced into it because of our work. I don't regret anything, Johnny. I'm not ashamed of anything and I don't regret anything. Even if— well, even if we had gone to bed together, I wouldn't be ashamed. Because you're a wonderful guy, Johnny. You're as wonderful and honest a guy as I ever hope to meet." She laughed a little in the middle of the drizzle of tears. "You're awfully attractive, too. The boy in Nebraska wears glasses, but I suppose that isn't important. The important thing is that I want him and I want the kind of life we would have together."

"Take it, Chloe. Grab it while there's still a chance for you."

"My feeling for you will never change, Johnny. Forty years from now, if I were to see you across the room, my heart would make that funny sinking motion and there would be butterflies in my stomach. Give me a handkerchief."

The handkerchief I took out from my pocket was stained with the blood I had wiped off the knife. I took a fresh one from my breast pocket. Chloe dabbed around her eyes. "I've said all those nice things about you, Maguire. Why don't you say something nice about me?"

"I wish I were like the guy in Nebraska," I said. "I wish that I could love someone like you, be right for her and be able to have her."

The cab stopped in front of Chloe's apartment. "I'll get out. Don't come up, please. I'm full of little butterflies and I don't think I ought to be. I won't see you again. I'm going to leave in the morning."

She held her hand for me to shake. "You're too damn well bred," I said, and pulled her lips against mine. I kissed her hard. "That's the way to say good-by, little one."

The words were whispered: "Good-by, Johnny."

I sat motionless and silent against the worn leather car seat until the sound of the cab driver blowing his nose woke me back to consciousness. He turned around and his eyes were red. "I ain't bawled since I was twelve years old," he said.

"You don't have to cry, Al. In a way, it's a happy ending."

"Where do you want to go now? Home?"

I thought for a minute and then gave him Tina's address.

Tina was going to be surprised as hell because all I wanted was a hot shower and to go to sleep for a long time. But I wanted the warm, comfortable feeling of someone lying beside me. I needed that. I was remembering what Chloe had been saying about loneliness.

"Drive faster, will you, Al?"

THE END